❦ The Long Ago Lake ❧

Mill Lake was a perfect lake.

The Long Ago Lake

A Book of Nature Lore and Crafts

by
MARNE WILKINS
with illustrations by Martha Weston

Chronicle Books / San Francisco

Published 1989 by Chronicle Books.

Originally published by Sierra Club Books.

Library of Congress Cataloging-in-Publication Data

Wilkins, Marne.
    The long ago lake : a book of nature lore and crafts by Marne Wilkins ; with illustrations by Martha Weston.
        p.   cm.
    Reprint, Originally published: San Francisco : Sierra Club Books, © 1978.
    Bibliography: p.
    Includes index.
    Summary: The author recollects her childhood summers in the Wisconsin Lakes district and the nature lessons her family learned from their Indian friends. Nature crafts projects are included.
    ISBN 0-87701-632-1
    1. Natural history — Outdoor books — Juvenile literature.
    2. Natural history — Wisconsin — Juvenile literature. 3. Handicraft — Juvenile literature. [1. Natural history — Wisconsin. 2. Nature craft. 3. Handicraft.] I. Weston, Martha, ill. II. Title.
    [QH48.W48 1990]
    508.775 — dc20
    [B]   89-32847
                                                          CIP
                                                          AC

10 9 8 7 6 5 4 3 2 1

Chronicle Books
275 Fifth Street
San Francisco, California
94103

For Liz and Muff and theirs.
To Al and Peg.

TABLE OF CONTENTS

A Long Time Ago
page 11

❧{ Part One }☙

Water: Worlds, Wonder, Knots, and Pots
page 25

❧{Part Two}❧

Meadows and Prairies: Flowers, Grass, Owls, and Howls
page 49

Soggy Bogs, 50; How to Build a Birdhouse, 51; Beautiful Treasures, 55; How to Make a Field I.D. Kit, 57; Learning from the Birds, 58; How to Preserve Flowers and Leaves, 60; How to Make a Grass Handle and More, 63; Red Rock Land, 65; How to Make a Tassel Doll, 66; The Runaway, 68; How to Build Rock Walls, 70; Belgians and Buffalo Chaps, 72; How to Make a Bird Feeding Station, 73; Everlasting Flowers, 76.

❧{Part Three}❧

Forests and Trees: Seeds, Pods, Needles, and Leaves
page 81

How to Make Things Using Seeds and Pods, 83; How to Make Shakes and Posts, 85; How to Make Prints, 86; A Log Cabin Adventure, 87; Snowballs and Robins' Eggs, 88; How to Make a Lashed Table, 90; Caught in a Ring of Fire, 94; How to Make a Wooden Spoon, 95; Wild Creatures and Us, 97; How to Make Casts of Tracks, 100; Keeping Track, 101; How to Make and Use Lichen Dye, 104; Colors from Plants, 105; How to Make a Pine Needle Basket, 107; The No-Peace Pipe, 109; How to Make Christmas Wreaths, 111; How to Make a Christmas Bird, 112.

❧{Part Four}❧

Sky Above: Wind, Clouds, Stars, and Sun
page 117

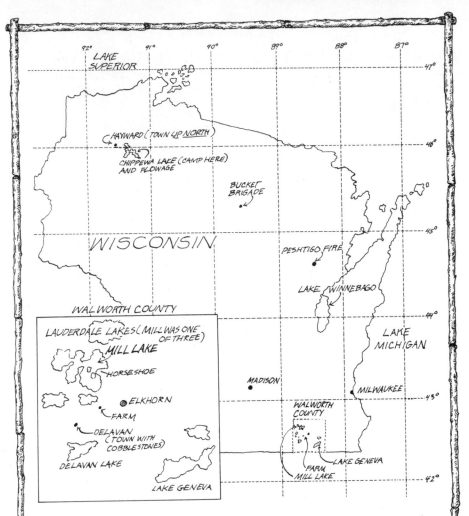

The stories and anecdotes in this book took place mostly when I was a girl in Wisconsin. I lived in a small town, but spent part of the year at my grandfather's farm, part of the year at the family house at Mill Lake, and a month each summer at the secret lake *up north*. Here is a map that shows where these places are. Now you know why streams and lakes were so much a part of our lives. We were surrounded by them.

{A Long Time Ago}

ONCE, A LONG TIME AGO, I was a young girl. I had a brother and three boy cousins, and we all grew up together. Our home was located in a small Wisconsin town which was surrounded by dairy farms, wood lots, and lakes. In the summertime we cousins and our mothers and fathers and grandparents all moved to the lake. Our lake, Mill Lake, was a very old one made when the glaciers pushed the land in Wisconsin around during the Ice Age. It was supplied with fresh water from many beautiful springs and from trickling little streams. The lake had a good flow of water to its outlet, and the Indians had built a mill there to grind grain many years before white settlers ever knew where Wisconsin was. Mill Lake was a perfect lake, and my cousins and brother and I would scrap with anyone who argued any other was better. Even though we loved Mill Lake, we looked forward to the month of August when we left it for awhile. It was then that we stuffed the family cars with everything needed to keep us warm and for catching fish, and we drove *up north*. We had a secret place and secret friends.

Shall I tell you? Well, my uncle is a fisherman, and he never gives up trying to find the best place to fish and the best way to do it. Michigan, Minnesota, and Wisconsin have a particular fish called a *muskie* that lives in northern lakes. Every year many huge muskies are caught and weighed to see which state produces the biggest fish. When my uncle was a young boy, he made friends with some Chippewa Indians who lived in the northern corner of Wisconsin. They told him of a hidden lake where he would be able to catch all the fish he could imagine — especially muskies. They invited him to their home and led him to that lake. They gave him permission to camp and fish there and that is where he took us. His Indian friend had children, too, and they became our friends.

We cousins always knew we had found the right trail to the Indians' secret lake because there was a giant lodgepole pine tree at the edge of the camp, and it could be seen from a long way. We scrambled out of the loaded cars as soon as they stopped and raced to the tree. Up we climbed to see who could reach the top first. One year we discovered we were getting *big*. No sooner had we reached our favorite sitting branch, which was large enough for all of us to sit on, than it snapped, and we tumbled out of the pine, bouncing, scraping, and crashing into a heap at the bottom in the merciful duff. The Chippewa boys had heard us arrive and were standing at the edge of the woods, holding their sides from laughing so hard! They instantly made up for it, though, by helping us gather a pail full of blueberries which my aunt then made into a pie and baked next to an open fire down by the lake.

Preparing the camp was a job we did carefully. We always made it so that when we left for home at summer's end, it was hardly possible to know anyone had been there. That way our camp stayed a special, secret, and wild place. When the ice was thick, the Indians would saw blocks of ice which they shared with us. We carefully dug holes and packed them with sawdust to keep the ice from melting and to keep the fish we caught cool and safe from bears.

How to Make a Reflector Oven

Materials needed: sheet metal or heavy-duty aluminum foil, tin shears.

The kind of blueberry pie Aunt Gladys made was a one crust version baked in a roasting pan lid. My mother and aunt were wizards at cooking during all kinds of weather and in all conditions. The two Coleman stoves were set up behind a big tarp against rain or wind, and most of our camp meals featured some product from their fires. Of course these stoves had ovens, but the oven we liked best was a simple reflector.

A successful reflector oven requires:

(1) A good steady hot-bedded fire.

(2) A way to mount your baking pan off the ground in front of the reflector.

(3) Shiny material to reflect the heat of the fire onto your baked goods.

Reflectors can be made of rock that is thoroughly heated but other materials work too. Sheet metal or tin is cut into a piece that is 2 feet by 2 feet and folded in the middle. A hole is punched in each of the four corners large enough to hold a coat hanger wire which is poked through and bent to pull the two halves together to form an angle.

If sides are needed, the original piece of metal is cut 4 feet long across the top half and 2 feet along the bottom. Then cut the side triangle down to the center fold. This should make a triangle about 12 inches by 12 inches by 17 inches from the top to the center fold.

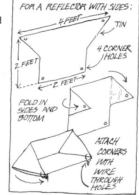

FOR A REFLECTOR WITH SIDES:
4 FEET
TIN
2 FEET
4 CORNER HOLES
2 FEET
FOLD IN SIDES AND BOTTOM
ATTACH CORNERS WITH WIRE THROUGH HOLES

The baked goods are placed on a rack of some kind so they are off the ground and between the reflector oven and the hot bed of coals. The reflector is adjusted, so that the heat from the fire is reflected onto the baked goods.

The whole oven can also be made by using heavy-duty aluminum foil bent over sticks for a frame. We like to carry foil on camping trips instead of other cooking utensils. There always seems to be a forked stick which, when covered, can be just the kind of pan you want to use.

BEND FOIL OVER STICKS

MOVE REFLECTOR CLOSER TO FOOD FOR MORE HEAT

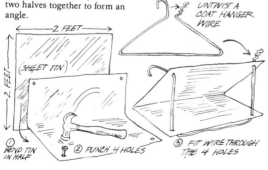

2 FEET
2 FEET
(SHEET TIN)
UNTWIST A COAT HANGER WIRE
① BEND TIN IN HALF
② PUNCH 4 HOLES
③ FIT WIRE THROUGH THE 4 HOLES

13

We tumbled out of the pine, crashing into a heap.

Fires were built on the sandy beach. And boxes holding food and gear were either hung by rope or lashed to trees to keep them away from animals.

{Outdoor Wisdom}

I have found out since growing up that no matter what kind of outdoor living you do, there are certain things you need to know. I have camped in snow, in high mountains, in deserts, along streams, and on islands, in crowded public campgrounds, and in wild, scary forests. Now I live in the wooded mountains of Northern California on a little ranch a long way from the small town and lake and farms where I grew up. Our Chippewa friends and my life in all these places have taught me so many tricks and habits to make living and camping out-of-doors enjoyable and interesting that I would like to share them with you.

First, there are two big, important habits that people can spend all their lives trying to learn well. It's true! And they will seem so simple you'll probably laugh, but — just the same — they come before anything else. The first is the habit of *seeing* what you look at. The Indians know that habit better than anybody and our Chippewa friends taught us what they could. It was hard to learn, though.

I'll tell you an example. Recently I was describing to a friend a beautiful fresh hide a man had given me to tan for leather. I was pleased with the pretty markings and had already begun to work on it. The friend asked me if the hide was prime. First, I was surprised and then I felt pretty stupid. I had not really *seen* that hide. I had looked only at the markings. Of course, anything but a newborn calf would not be a very good hide in the summer, so I hurried home to look. But luckily enough, the inside was snowy white and unmarked by any stains or streaks. It was a prime hide. I had

15

spent several hours scraping and salting that side of the hide, but I never did really *see* it. It's strange, isn't it? Sometimes it is hard to *see* what you look at. In the out-of-doors, it is so important that sometimes it not only saves you a whole lot of trouble, but maybe even your life.

The other habit you need to learn to be a really good outdoor person is to *be ready*. That means having your food planned; you tools sharp, clean, and safe; and your gear in good condition. To me, it means even more than that; it means *being ready* to do the most important things. *Being ready* means when somebody says, "Let's go fishing," I not only know where my pole is, but I know how to fish, too. My dad understood that. He used to put a pail in the backyard for us to practice casting into. If we were *ready,* we could hit the water in the pail every time. Then when we did go fishing, we could cast our lure into the water right by a lily pad or stump so that a wise, worthy fish might think it was just exactly what he wanted for dinner that day. *Be ready,* and you will know what knot to use when you want to tie a packsaddle onto a horse. *Be ready,* and if you need to start a fire during a rainstorm you can do it. If you go too far from home, and it gets dark too early, *be ready* to find your way home with the help of the stars.

Learning to *be ready* will teach you many things. You can enjoy learning the knots for making nets and securing loads, and how to lash and whip rope, or how to tell time by the sun, or when a storm is approaching by the clouds and the feel of the wind. You can practice listening to sounds and warnings all around you. For example, do you know what the ground squirrel is scolding about? And why? Is it a snake after quail eggs? Or a hawk overhead? Why is the blue jay squawking so loudly? Is he worried? About what? Listen to the trees. Often you can tell by the changing sounds what the weather is doing. Rocks tumbling onto a mountain path in little trickles can be a warning that an animal just scurried away above

16

{How to Tie Some Useful Knots}

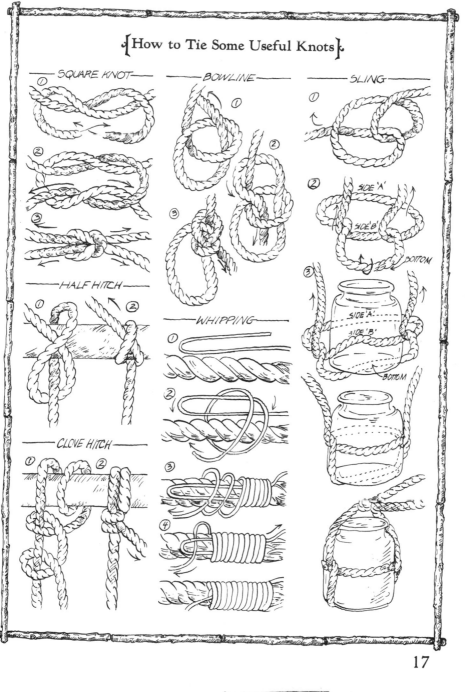

SQUARE KNOT

BOWLINE

SLING

① ② ③

SIDE 'A'
SIDE 'B'
BOTTOM

SIDE 'A'
SIDE 'B'
BOTTOM

HALF HITCH

① ②

WHIPPING

① ② ③ ④

CLOVE HITCH

① ②

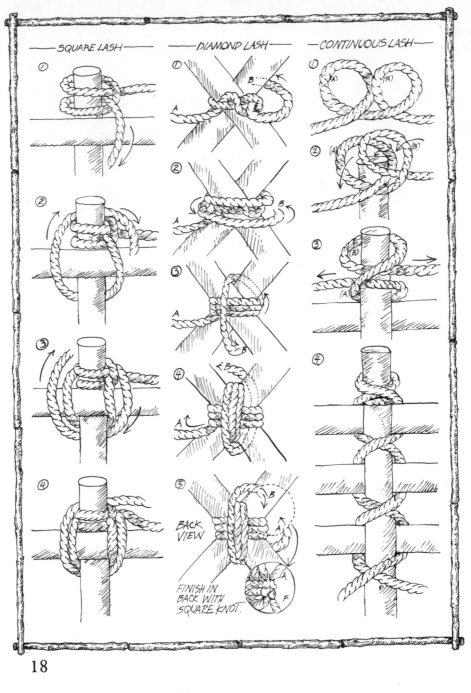

SQUARE LASH — DIAMOND LASH — CONTINUOUS LASH

BACK VIEW

FINISH IN BACK WITH SQUARE KNOT.

you, or it may mean that a bigger slide started somewhere higher up. *Be ready* to see the little rocks and read what they can tell you. *Be ready* to know what animals live near you and how they live, so you won't hurt them in their homes, and they won't accidently hurt you either. You can learn to read tracks and how to *see* nests and burrows, too. Many animals leave droppings, or scats, that tell us who they are and what they have eaten. In some scats, you will see feathers, pellets, down, or broken eggshells, if you practice looking.

⸱{ Ghost Owl and Mountain Cat }⸱

There is a wonderful man named Dr. Allen, an ornithologist at Cornell University, who loves birds and has told us many things about them. He has made records of bird sounds, and they have helped me to learn more about birds I couldn't recognize before. Now each evening about five o'clock I hear an owl conversation. The owls talk back and forth, calling across several hills. By listening to Dr. Allen's recording, I finally decided which owl it was that I could hear.

One night our family saw what appeared to be a huge flying ghost sailing and swooping toward some trees where our chickens were roosting. We were *ready*. We knew from listening and comparing with Dr. Allen's recordings that some rare great horned owls lived nearby, and that someday they would tire of catching mice and try a nice fat hen instead. We turned a bright lantern right at the hen's tree and away the owl soared. He was huge, but we were *ready* for his visit, and so we saved our hen.

Up north at the secret lake, we used to listen to the loons laugh and call. Their sound was so spooky we shivered. We soon learned that it was when they didn't call that we should be afraid. When they hid, we should do the same! Back down

19

Preparing the camp was a job we did carefully.

at Mill Lake, we would be gliding along in a canoe when suddenly all chatter among the red-winged blackbirds would stop. We stoped and listened, too, Then we saw that mink had come down to hunt by the water or that hawks were flying too close.

One time my own little girl and I were hiking on a high cliff trail. Going around a ledge, we came to a high overhang making a space like a cave. We had already noticed what seemed to be the fresh tracks of a mountain cat, and we had decided just how we would leave that trail in a hurry if we had to. Sure enough, right there in that cave was a freshly killed rabbit, a perfect mountain-cat lunch; but there was no cat! We just knew that cat was in a safe place watching us. We were *ready,* and we left the trail as we had planned to, so the cat didn't have to be afraid of us stealing its lunch; and we had nothing to fear, either.

Besides *being ready* and learning to *see,* some other important skills and habits have to do with eating and sleeping. Whenever we find ourselves out-of-doors, different conditions determine how we do those two things. Learning to prepare, carry, and store food and gear, and to make a comfortable place to sleep can be a pretty sizable task out-of-doors. Other know-how has to do with finding your way, sometimes by the stars, sometimes by a compass, or sometimes by reading tracks or maps. And more has to do with finding ways to help people, animals, and plants, and learning new things from them. There is no end to all the things we can learn about and do outdoors!

{Part One}

WATER
Worlds, Wonder, Knots, and Pots

AY or early June was when we moved to Mill Lake for the summer. As soon as we arrived, we cousins all ran down the hill to the water. That started our annual inspection tour. In the whooping and shouting and excitement, one of us would always slip and roll most of the way down, barely stopping in time at the breakwater. Bob would balance on the rocks at the edge of the lake and, more times than I can count, would lose his glasses in the icy water. The rest of the day we invented ways to fish for them without getting wet. At least once that day somebody would come and insist that our energies were needed for unloading supplies. But after making sure that the big tins of marshmallows and cartons of graham crackers were stored on their top shelves, we found more important things to do.

We hung the swings and hammocks. We checked the boathouse for swallow nests, the pier for ice damage, and grandfather's peony bed for a proper supply of ants. Grandfather's father had brought the first peonies to our town when he came from England. Grandfather insisted that ants were necessary to help the peony buds to open. Since his peonies were always spectacular, he was no doubt right.

{How to Make a Rush Mat}

Materials needed: cattail (bulrush) leaves, masking tape, scissors.

Gather young cattail rushes (leaves) and dry them, out of the sun. When you are ready to weave, dampen and wrap them in a towel. Use 18 rushes, each about 1 inch wide and 30 inches long for the long side and 14 rushes about 26 inches long for the short side.

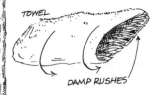

TOWEL

DAMP RUSHES

Cut the bottom end to the same shape as the top end with scissors. Now lay the long rushes out flat, side by side, with no space in between. You can keep them in place with a piece of masking tape across the ends.

FIRST RUSH: OVER FIRST, THEN UNDER

SECOND RUSH: UNDER FIRST, THEN OVER

To begin weaving your mat, start at one side with a short rush and work opposite the direction of the long rushes. Put the short one first *over* then *under* the 18 long rushes. The next short rush is placed beside the the first short rush, but it starts by going *under* the first long rush, then over, under, over, under.

Leave 6 inches sticking out at the top and bottom of the mat and at each end. These are turned back and woven into the other weaving so that the edge of the mat has a solid finish instead of a loose, wiggly one.

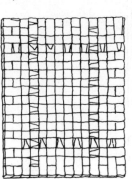

If you want to make a square mat, use rushes that are all the same length. If you want to make a thicker one, use two layers and weave them as one.

How many different kinds of water can you think about? Rushing streams, big rivers, lakes, reservoirs, ponds, oceans, lagoons, and many more? Then do you think about beaches and swamps and marshes and cliffs and caves and jettys and bogs and currents and riptides and quicksand and sunburn? And what about shells and weeds and sand and fleas and jiggers and nests and turtles and pollywogs and bullfrogs and lily pads and beavers and bears? Do you think about swimming? Sailing? Canoeing or speedboating? Water-skiing or scuba diving or surfing? What about fishing? Do you need a pole, a net, a trap? Do you use bait, a lure, a fly?

No matter what kind of water or where it is, there is one rule to know from the start. The rule is that we must treat water with respect. One false move, one little breath taken at the wrong time, and water can be a very dangerous place. Mostly water is wonderful, full of adventure and teeming with living things and great beauty. It is a world for enjoying, if you remember that one rule.

{The Horseshoe}

One of the most perfect worlds at the lake was the part known as the Horseshoe — because of its shape, I suppose. It had slow-moving water and bogs and lily pads and frogs and turtles. It had rushes and sand bars, perfect for secret picnics. A canoe or raft could slide around all day without being noticed in the busy world there. In spring the rushes could be pulled up for tasty roots, more delicious than any potato! When the rush leaves were dry, they could be used to weave pretty mats and pads for grandma's table. We had contests to see who could pull the longest lily stem without tipping the canoe over, and we enjoyed presenting our gorgeous trophies for bouquets at home. No one ever tired of their beauty.

(*Text continued on page 30.*)

{ How to Make a Rope Swing }

Materials needed: ¾-inch or thicker cotton rope, rubber tire (optional).

A sturdy ¾-inch cotton rope of the sort used for leading horses is the safest for this swing, because cotton won't burn when it slides over hands and knees. Other ropes may be stronger and weather better, but they burn and stretch.

The rope is simply slung over a high but strong tree branch and fastened with a clove hitch. (See Knots page 17.) Overhand knots are tied at intervals down its length, giving a grip for feet and hands and making quick climbing and swinging an adventure. You can put the overhand knots in before you tie your rope to the branch.

We also had swings made of rope that was tied to a rubber tire and one great swing that was made from a saddle tied in such a way that when you mounted the saddle, you rode a mildly bucking bronco.

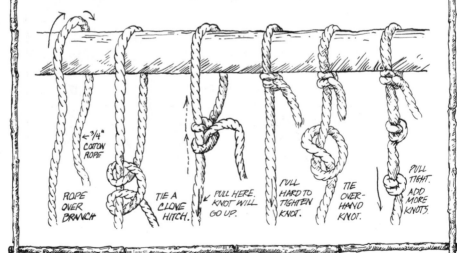

ROPE OVER BRANCH

← ¾" COTTON ROPE

TIE A CLOVE HITCH.

PULL HERE. KNOT WILL GO UP.

PULL HARD TO TIGHTEN KNOT.

TIE OVER-HAND KNOT.

PULL TIGHT. ADD MORE KNOTS.

We hung the swings and hammocks.

One summer a dredge came to "clean out" the Horseshoe to make room for more swimmers and boats. Now there isn't a lily anywhere — or a bulrush either.

There was a stream which fed the lake that went through a farm, and the farm pasture came right down to the edge of the lake. The stream had thick grass growing down over its edges and all kinds of creatures lived in the sheltered world under that grass. We made dams that created ponds, and we watched as young turtles grew up in them. They were our summer family and we gave them names and built houses for them out of rock and willow sticks.

One thing I learned there about water was that it always wants to get under things, and it always moves to somewhere if it can.

It was a shock to me to learn that the Indians used baskets to cook in — even to boil water in. I knew people who couldn't even cook in nice steel kettles, but cooking in a basket I thought must be magic. Only later did I discover the secrets. To cook the food in baskets, the Indians used rocks which had been heated in the fire, then dropped into the basket of food or water. But how did they keep water from getting out the holes? I have learned since then that water also goes into air spaces in certain materials like clay and wood and grass and causes them to swell and become larger. People have put this knowledge to use, letting the water itself make holes and seams grow tight. That is how a wooden barrel works. It is also one way a basket can be made to hold water. This is how rawhide leather can be made strong and how wood can be shaped into curves that are unnatural to it.

Another thing that happens when water goes into material like clay is that once it fills up all the air spaces, it sometimes starts going on through. An Indian person I know irrigates his garden with clay pots, just like all his people did before him. He makes a nice big pot out of clay that is porous. That means it has a lot of air spaces. The pot is then fired until it is

30

How to Make a Clay Pot

Materials needed: clay — earthenware (can be dug up or bought), large spoon, cloth.

Pots may be made in several different ways or in combinations. They are either built by hand or thrown on a potter's wheel. This clay pot is hand built and requires no tools, except perhaps a spoon. It is made by the coil method. Make up the clay to be moist enough to handle and shape without it sticking to your hands. Then work the clay roughly, to get all the air holes out of it.

Pinch off a handful and begin to roll between the palms of your hands to form a snakelike strip. As the strip becomes longer, put it on a smooth surface and roll it until it's of the same thickness along its full length, as thick as a finger, about ½ inch. Make several strips and keep them damp by covering them with a wet cloth.

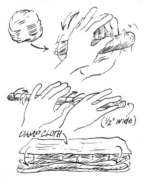

DAMP CLOTH

½" WIDE

The bottom may be made by patting a piece of clay to a round with a thickness of 3/8 inch and a diameter of about 4 inches.

4"

3/8" HIGH

POT BOTTOM

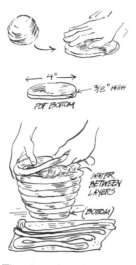

WATER BETWEEN LAYERS

(BOTTOM)

The coils are then wound around the base, adding water to join the coils to each other. One coil is added on top of another in this manner until the desired height and shape are made. To make a smooth surface, the clay from the top coil is gently pulled down onto the coil below it by thumb pressure. This results in a sure seal between the coils but is still

USE OPPOSITE PRESSURE

not smooth. To smooth, wet the clay until the surface feels creamy and use the back of a spoon to shape the clay into a smooth surface.

When working a pot, it's necessary to use *opposite* pressure. This means that as you work on the outside surface, you put equal pressure on the inside surface just opposite the place you are working. This helps prevent losing the shape as you work. Shape the pot by adding shorter or longer coils to make wider or narrower places in the pot.

When you get to the top, moisten the edge of the top clay coil and flatten it into a smooth

WET TOP COIL, SMOOTH FLAT

WET POT

SMOOTH SIDES WITH SPOON BACK

surface. Put the pot to one side to dry until it is leather hard. Then clean off rough places and pare (or cut) the bottom if it seems too thick, especially where it joins the coils. Let it dry thoroughly before firing.

How to Fire a Clay Pot at Home

Materials needed: firewood, brick, pebbles, clay pot.

There are two methods for firing without a kiln. One is in the fireplace and the other is out-of-doors.

I try to thoroughly warm the pot before firing it in the fireplace. This allows me to start with a bed of hot coals and ashes instead of a cold fireplace.

PRE-WARMED POT TO BE FIRED
PEBBLES
HOT COALS AND ASHES
BRICK
— FIREPLACE —

The pot may be set on a brick in the middle of these. You may want to mount your pot on a few small, flat pebbles placed on the brick to allow some circulation under the pot.

HOT-BURNING KINDLING
2 HOURS STEADY HEAT

Now carefully build a fire of fine, hot-burning wood over your pot. Add more wood as the fire requires, building up as much heat as possible, while keeping as little fire as you can balance. Try to keep the temperature even for two hours or more. It is best to do the firing at night because this allows the pot to cool in the fireplace overnight.

Take it out in the morning, carefully removing debris and ashes. A dry paint brush will clean off the ash dust. If your

clay did not contain too much iron, your pot will probably be very satisfactory for many uses.

A high iron content tends to make pots brittle and difficult to handle. Often you can tell at a glance by the sparkle and very red look of the fired clay if it has a lot of iron. Near my home, the natural potting clay that can be dug up is green, brown, or yellow, but all three fire to a deep terra cotta red — iron!

Open firing outside is similar to a fireplace but allows more flexibility. The traditional pottery of many countries is fired out-of-doors, and there are great variations in technical skills from crude to excellent. The Japanese have carried the quick-fire outdoor method to extreme refinement, and it is known as the *raku* method.

— OUTDOOR FIRING —

PRE-WARMED POTS TO BE FIRED
BRICKS AND FUEL

A simple firing outside can be done over a pit or on level ground. In either case, the pots are carefully arranged in a pile of fuel with as little surface touching between them as is possible while still achieving a steady stack. Lightweight sticks are heaped on the pottery and kindled, and the fire is encouraged and tended for about two hours.

2 HOURS STEADY HEAT
LIGHT STICKS HEAPED ON

Warming the pots is a good idea, and a separate little smoldering fire can be made and kept going for this. Old pieces of broken pottery can be placed on top of the stack for some protection against cool drafts.

The main idea is to get as much heat and circulation evenly around the pots as possible. Finishing is the same as with fireplace firing.

Bernard Leach, who wrote *A Potter's Book*, relates that he saw Nigerians heap dry grass on the embers at the end of a firing to prevent breakage from drafts. This is probably a good idea, as it is important in firing to bring the heat up gradually and cool it down gradually too. A draft of air that is a different temperature could easily crack the pot.

32

hard. Sometimes holes are added around the sides but not always. The pots are then buried at measured spaces throughout the garden, but the tops show just above ground. When they are filled with water, the water seeps slowly out through the holes and through the clay and feeds the garden plants nearby. When the pots are empty, the gardener knows it is time to water again, so he fills the pots. Many places in our country have good clay soil that can be made into nice pottery. It's not surprising that the remains of very ancient pots and different methods for making them can be found nearly everywhere.

People have always tried to find ways to store and carry water, and their inventions are as different as can be. Once when I was a little girl and on a visit to New Mexico, I was given a ten gallon hat. I didn't really believe that the cowboy hat was supposed to be named for how much water it carried; however, years later, I discovered that my tall hat did indeed hold a big drink for me and my horse. I was glad for it too!

It is important to know how to carry water and keep it cool because it is not always possible to be near good, safe drinking water. People who do long hours of work out-of-doors have come up with some beautiful methods. One of them is the practice of covering bottles or canteens so as to insulate them against sun or body heat. There are many ways to do this, from simply wrapping wet canvas or blanket material around water containers to the elegant and traditional demijohns which are made of knots or wicker closely covering the form of the bottle or canteen. Some of the most interesting demijohns are those made by sailors — always good knot makers — for their stored bottles of fresh water.

One time I tried and tried to find a person who could show me how to make a demijohn and had almost decided it was a lost art. Then I met a wonderful old German sheepherder who had been a sailor when he was a young man. He lent me a book on knots and in it were pictures of demijohns and

33

descriptions of the knots used for each! To my surprise, they were the most common knots, but made so tightly and neatly that they seemed different. The finishing touch on these was the top, which was a cork with a handle made out of a lovely shell. When I told my friend what I had found in his book, he became interested and showed me some other grand knots from his sailoring days.

There seems to be no end to the usefulness of knots and the different ways you can make them. Can you believe that the very same knots are used for making dainty necklaces and dress trimmings as are used for tying big loads onto trucks? The difference is the size of the material used, from fine cord to thick rope.

It wasn't long after this that I had a sick ewe, and my same friend came to help me with her. He saw that she needed to be raised into a standing position and between us we quickly rigged up a fine sling using a simple combination of broomsticks, gunny sacks, and a good rope.

When you live on a ranch or farm or if you like to spend a lot of time camping and hiking, sooner or later you will want to know how to make a litter. Litters are second cousins to slings because they are designed to move big loads. As with slings, you can use litters for raising an animal or a person or a load. But you can also carry the load because a litter is movable.

⁌ Mother and the Snakes ⁍

Have you ever become too tired when you have spent a day or a vacation by the water? It's the very best tiredness there is. At the lake I would lie for long hours, face down, looking through the pier boards and watching the schools of fish and the muskrat who lived under there. If I became too hot, I would slide off into the water and squish along to the

{How to Make a Demijohn}

Materials needed: seine twine or jute, bottle, scissors.

There are many ways to cover bottles. The easiest way is to start by covering the bottom itself and working out and then up. This consists of putting on a series of half hitches.

Begin by making a length of chain and hitching the ends together to make a small circle as shown. Then tuck the starting end under, and with the other end make hitches around the knot circle through the loops of the chain that is already there.

When you reach the edge of the bottle, pull your knots up, and keep them tight to make the turn. Then continue knotting up the sides of the bottle. When the hitches begin to come close

5.

REPEAT UNTIL CHAIN IS THE DESIRED LENGTH

6.

together as the bottle tapers, skip a loop at intervals.

Finish by weaving the end into the knotting. If the cord begins to fray while you are working, you can rub a piece of beeswax along the length of it. As you run out of twine, add more by tying on a new piece and either bury the knot or incorporate it into the hitches.

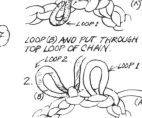

TO ADD ROWS TO CHAIN:

1.

(B) (A)

LOOP 1

LOOP (B) AND PUT THROUGH TOP LOOP OF CHAIN.

2.

LOOP 2   LOOP 1

(B)   (A)

PUT (B) THROUGH NEXT LOOP OF CHAIN TO MAKE LOOP 2

3.

LOOP 2

LOOP 1

(B)   (A)

PUT LOOP 2 THROUGH LOOP 1 AND PULL 1 CLOSED

(B)   LOOP 2

LOOP 1

(A)

LOOP 3

MAKE LOOP 3 WITH (B). CONTINUE, REPEATING STEPS 3 AND 4.

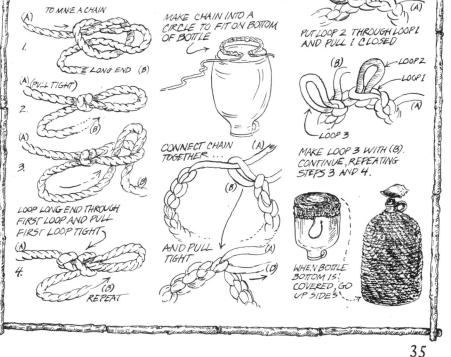

TO MAKE A CHAIN

(A)

1.

LONG END (B)

(A) (PULL TIGHT)

2.

(B)

(A)

3.

(B)

LOOP LONG END THROUGH FIRST LOOP AND PULL FIRST LOOP TIGHT.

(A)

4.

(B)

REPEAT

MAKE CHAIN INTO A CIRCLE TO FIT ON BOTTOM OF BOTTLE

CONNECT CHAIN TOGETHER ...   (A)

(B)

AND PULL TIGHT   (A)

(B)

WHEN BOTTLE BOTTOM IS COVERED, GO UP SIDES

{How to Make a Litter or Travois}

Materials needed: two poles, a blanket.

Two poles slipped through coat sleeves and the coat wrapped around and buttoned can make an emergency carrier. Another carrier that two people can manage is one made by using two strong poles laid side by side about 2 feet apart and on top of the middle third of a blanket or tarpaulin.

One side of the blanket is folded over a pole toward the middle; the second pole is placed over the blanket edge; and then the other third of the blanket folds over all, so it is three thicknesses of blanket and two poles.

Each person carrying holds the pole ends, and if the load being carried is a person, the rule is to carry feet first except uphill.

A one-man litter is made so that one end is dragged on the ground. It can be made by lashing either two poles together at one end or by putting a third pole across the end. The blanket or tarpaulin is then mounted like the two-man carrier, or it can be tied at the four corners, if the load is light enough.

This kind is easiest to use where it is sandy, like the beach. It makes a good emergency carrier for gear you find just too heavy when you're all sunburned and tired out.

POLES LASHED TOGETHER

LITTER FOR ONE CARRIER

POLES

BLANKET

LITTER FOR TWO CARRIERS

boathouse. Soft crabs and clams lived there, and there were great spiders to poke at. If the swallows were nesting at the boathouse, we stayed out. We didn't even put our boat away because swallows ruled there, and no one was allowed to enter without getting pecked!

Another cousin came from Texas to visit in the summer. He taught me how to catch snakes because he collected them. We learned about all the snakes that lived around us at the lake, where their homes were, and what they ate. I was going to make a collection too, but I wasn't much of a scientist. One day I found three nice snakes, but I was in a hurry to go swimming, so I wrapped them snugly in a bandanna and put them into my dresser drawer. The next thing we all heard was a yowl and a crash! My unsuspecting mother had opened my drawer to put the laundry away, and the three snakes were there to greet her. She fainted dead away! That ended my collection, but after my cousin went home, I mailed him three special snakes in a carefully made cage-box. He wrote and thanked me for *the* snake, and that was how I learned that king snakes eat other snakes — even rattlers. Since my "Texas cousin" summer, I have continued to see snakes. They are probably some of the most beautiful creatures on earth.

The little pools that you can find around the rocky places at the edges of lakes and streams and oceans are often treasure troves. Some of them are like old junkyards because of the empty shells and bits of bones and lures that float into them and stay trapped there. These pools are exquisite miniature worlds, and hours can be spent watching all the wiggling, busy things going on. The colors are often spectacular in these pools because of the weeds that grow in them. Twice I have seen the sapphire blue snake there. It is like finding the rarest and most costly jewel. In gold country the pools are where gold nuggets, which are heavy, settle under rocks until the next high water comes to the creeks.

No one was allowed to enter the boathouse without getting pecked.

At Mill Lake there were special pools created by the springs and bogs. The springs that fed the lake bubbled up in one little bay, and each spring was surrounded by boggy things that were half floating weed and half land. If we were feeling brave and rowdy, we would take a canoe paddle and shove it against the mass. The mass would part and move, but then it would come right back again. That was spooky and it wasn't hard to imagine all kinds of mysterious things under there. The plants in bogs are strange. Bogs are one place where you can even find several kinds of plants that eat insects for nourishment.

Sometimes pieces of the bogs broke loose and floated off until they snagged on a shallow place to become surprise islands! I was always a little afraid to get on one to explore. One time, when we arrived at camp up at the secret lake a bog island settled against our secluded beach. It was a rather large one with a couple of trees on it. One day my brother and cousins climbed one of those trees and rocked back and forth until the bog actually started to make waves. I was sure I'd never see them again and ran, wailing, up the hill for help!

The crystal clear water of the springs plus their bubbling created pockets of scoured sand, and the sun shone down in these pockets, lighting them and making them more beautiful than anyone could describe. Nothing lived in those pockets of very cold spring water, but the areas around them teemed with life, and there we caught big orange-bottomed turtles and slippery frogs and water spiders.

⟨Indian Secrets⟩

Our Chippewa friends told us about lake bottoms and some of their mysteries, which are pretty dramatic in glacier country like our part of Wisconsin. When the glacial ice

(*Text continued on page 43.*)

39

{How to Make Bone and Shell Jewelry}

Materials needed: bones, deer antlers, clam shells, hack saw, awl or ice pick, emery cloth, hand drill, coping saw.

Bone may be used either uncooked or cooked. A beef or ham bone works well. It must be cleaned of all grease, sinew, marrow, and flesh. To do this, scrape and then wash it thoroughly with detergent. Rinse and boil the bone in clean water or soak for a few days in warm water. Wood ash may be stirred into the water when soaking; the ash acts as a mild bleach. Dry the bone and cut it with a fine-toothed saw to the shape you want to use.

SCRAPE BONE CLEAN

RINSE BONE. SOAK IN WARM WATER A FEW DAYS. (ADD WOOD ASH AS A BLEACH)

A friend made a fine fleshing tool for me using a bone chewed on by a neighbor's dog and left, bleaching in the sun. It was a shank bone, hard as a rock, clean and hollow.

It fit my hand perfectly, so he cut the bottom edge into many sawlike teeth. It is a fine tool for cleaning hides.

Small bones, such as bird bones, may be strung on a fine thong into patterns combined with beads and shells. Chicken bones that are cooked should not be used as they are too soft. Animal bones may be polished with sandpaper or emery cloth, carved with designs to look like ivory, and used for pendents, bolo ties, or buttons.

I like to keep a supply of bone buttons for the garments that I weave. Deer antlers make good

HACK SAW

BONE

AWL, FOR CARVING DESIGN (ICE PICK WOULD WORK)

EMERY CLOTH TO POLISH BONE

buttons. Every once in a while I find one that has been shed in the woods, or a hunter friend will give me one to use.

Saw through the antler to the thickness desired, just as you would saw frozen sausage. An antler button is usually less than a ¼ inch. Polish the piece with pumice or emery cloth, and drill two or four holes for sewing the button on.

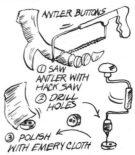

ANTLER BUTTONS

① SAW ANTLER WITH HACK SAW
② DRILL HOLES
③ POLISH WITH EMERY CLOTH

Clam shells make nice buttons too. They can be easily sawed into a small, round shape. Drilling sometimes splits them, but if you work carefully, holes can be made.

CUT CLAM SHELLS WITH COPING SAW

Deer and elk antlers are treasured teething devices for puppies. One time a friend gave me some elk buttons for Christmas. When we came to the tree on Christmas morning, things were in shambles. Our collie had smelled the buttons and ransacked the packages until he found them. He must have remembered his puppy days. To me the buttons looked and smelled just like regular ivory ones!

40

I was almost sure I'd never see them again.

⟨How to Make a Tom-Tom⟩

Materials needed: a hollow log or container; rawhide, chamois, sheepskin or inner tube rubber; lacing.

An Indian drum can be made from many things such as oatmeal boxes or nail kegs with the top and bottom covered with rubber inner tubing or even heavy paper.

If you can find a hollow log about a foot in diameter, cut a section out of it about 14 inches long, clean it out, and scrape any loose bark from the outside.

CLEAN OUT HOLLOW LOG → SCRAPE OFF LOOSE BARK
14"

The top and bottom may be made of rawhide, chamois, sheepskin, or inner tube rubber. Cut two pieces; one for the top and the other for the bottom. Cut the piece large enough so that some of the material folds down over the sides about 2 to 3 inches.

Lay the circles out flat, and punch holes around the circle at even spaces, 1 inch from the edge.

Put one piece on the floor; place the hollow wood on top of

② CUT 2 CIRCLES FOR TOP AND BOTTOM

(COULD BE RAWHIDE, INNER TUBE RUBBER, CHAMOIS OR SHEEPSKIN.)

③

PUNCH HOLES 1 INCH FROM EDGE IN EACH CIRCLE.

this. Put the second circle over the top. Using a leather shoelace thong, lace the two circles together, going from top to bottom in a zigzag (one up, one down). Keep the lacing as snug as possible. The thong will stretch over the wood sides, making a triangle pattern.

④
2" or 3"

⑤ LACE TOP AND BOTTOM TIGHTLY, LIKE THIS

RAWHIDE THONG

⑥ KNOT THONG. TAP KNOT FLAT.

When you knot the thong at the end, take a mallet or hammer and tap the knot flat. When it is all laced and secure, thoroughly soak the top and bottom leathers and thong with water and allow to dry. They should be quite tight. If not, wet them again or adjust the lacing. Flattening the knots of the leather thong will keep them tight.

⑦ SOAK TOP, BOTTOM, AND THONG WITH WATER....

.... WHEN LEATHER DRIES, IT WILL STRETCH TIGHT.

scraped the land, it cut through layers of soil and water. Sometimes what appears to be a bottomless lake is the result of those cuts, which actually connect two or more lakes by underground rivers. The Indians told us that objects which were lost in one lake sometimes were found in another because of those underground waterways. They used to know all the best places for finding treasures, and they made beautiful jewelry and beads and buttons from polished shells, horns, and bones that they had found.

While we shared many hours with those friends and with their help learned about the woods and lakes *up north,* there were some things we were never a part of and never shared. In the bark and log cabins of the Indian village, we had seen beautiful decorated buckskin ceremonial dresses. Head-pieces, breastplates, and drums were all made and kept for special events. We were friends, yet we never went at night to the village events where those special, decorated garments were worn. Sometimes in the nearest town there were programs in the park which were supposed to be true Indian dances, but I am sure they were not. The garments used in the park dances were different, but also pretty.

I can remember the very first time I heard that village ceremony. A body of water causes sounds and voices to carry farther than the same sounds would carry over land. I had been tucked snugly into my bedroll for the night and was sleeping soundly. Suddenly I became aware of a sound I had never heard before. The moon was bright in the sky. It was reflecting on the water so the whole world was brilliant in its silver light. I first wondered if the sound was an animal that makes a special noise on such a night, and I shivered with a cold feeling brought on by fear of what is unknown. My eyes strained, peering into the light and shadows. Gradually my ears sorted out the sounds. *Tom-toms!* I had made and played with tom-toms, but to me they were just play drums. These were the real thing. Voices began to separate from the

43

I could hear the sounds of the ceremony clear and resounding.

drums, and I could hear a chant. It was all from another world; the Indian world we could never enter. That was a world known only to them and their ancestors. All I could do was sink back into my blankets and be glad we were friends, that the warpath days were over, and that water was near us so I could hear the sounds of the ceremony, clear and resounding and never to be forgotten.

{Part Two}

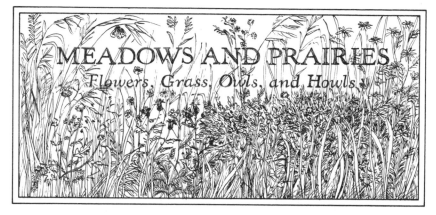

MEADOWS AND PRAIRIES
Flowers, Grass, Owls, and Howls

Y brother and cousins and I used to have long and serious debates about what we thought was the best place in the world. The boys usually claimed a place in the woods or by a lake was, but I almost always defended the meadows — deep, grassy, flowering meadows — springtime meadows, summertime or anytime meadows.

On the first day of May each year, my whole family headed for the meadows to gather flowers for our May baskets. We had made little baskets in advance and had precious friends to whom we gave our buttercups, shooting stars, and lilies. The tradition was to leave a basket on the doorstep, ring the bell, then run. If your friend caught you, you were kissed! Besides those adventures, we took May baskets to old people who couldn't get out to join us and to sick friends, too. May Day was a happy day, marking the end of winter snow and cold and promising warm spring and summer days to come.

For all the creatures who had been living under snow-heaped thickets or in burrows and nests underground, sunny May meant having grass and tender shoots and roots to eat. For birds it was a hectic time of declaring territories and getting settled and building new nests.

49

The meadows and prairie land that surrounded our spring-fed, natural lakes were a wonderful world. As I grew up I learned that meadows and prairies extend clear across our country with vast expanses opening up in the West. I learned there are many kinds of meadows too, but all prairies and meadows are wide open. You can run and stretch and shout and fill yourself with sunshine and air, and you can see and see and see — up and down and all around. Cows and horses and sheep use them for pastures; birds and small animals makes nests and burrows in them. Little streams feed them and carve them; and solitary, monumental trees decorate them like sculptures. Wild meadows and prairies have deer, antelope, and elk in them; and I have seen herds, startled by a sudden sound, run like the wind and never stop as far as I could see. Our own meadows, where I live now, welcome our colts and lambs and are sunshiny, grassy, perfect new worlds for them.

The edges of meadows make prime hiding and nesting places. They have thickets of wild rose briar, willows, berries, and sometimes even lumpy places with big rocks, which provide lookouts for birds and animals and forts for boys and girls.

⊰[Soggy Bogs]⊱

Marshes are found between meadows and lakes, ponds and streams. Back home, some of our marshes had peat bogs in them. We were always concerned that they would start burning. They did this once in a while, because in the decaying process so much heat was given off that a fire sometimes started by itself. Marshes are just the opposite of meadows. They aren't open at all. Instead of being able to run and run, you must pick your way carefully, always with a fear that you might make a mistake and so fall into the tangly, watery

⚓[How to Build a Birdhouse]⚓

Materials needed; nails, 2 inches of ¼-inch dowel, screw eye, 46-inch piece of 1-x-6-inch lumber.

All over the country people build birdhouses to attract birds to their gardens for their songs and company, and for help catching insects which harm the garden. Birds, like people, have certain ideas about what a proper house should provide, and one of the most important features of all is the size of the entrance opening.

The most well-known are: house wrens — 7/8 inch; white-breasted nuthatches — 1 1-1/4 inches; woodpeckers — 2 inches; martins and tree swallows — 2 inches; house finches — 2 inches; and chickadees — 1 1/8 inches. Robins like a more open place than a house. They will come to a roost that has only two sides. Some birds, such as martins, enjoy living in colonies like apartment dwellers; others would rather be alone.

One time I watched and listened as a wren and a goldfinch argued about a piece of wool the wren had tried to stuff into a house. Later he chose another house and abandoned the wool as well as the original house. However, when a goldfinch decided to take the wool, the wren "said" no.

All morning they carried on a chirping argument. Finally they moved to a neutral corner of the yard, and there the wren perched, never taking his eye off the goldfinch, as the goldfinch flew back, snatched the wool, and stuffed it quickly into his nest in a rose bush. Then the wren sang his little raspy banjo song and went on about his business.

I think it is important for birdhouses to have a sturdy perch under their entrance as birds very often bring food only to the door and thrust it in to the nesting mate; or else they land, look around, and then enter.

The entrance must face opposite prevailing winds, if possible. One of the most crucial times in a bird's life is the moment it leaves the nest. If the nest is in a birdhouse, other predator birds often have noticed the action as the house swings when the wriggling babies grow and become noisier and noisier. You can know when to help by paying attention. Parent birds must coax their babies to come out, and you will notice a very different, insistent note in their calls. Also, they don't dive into the house with food when they are calling like that.

If you have placed the house so that it is safe from animals who steal from nests, your next concern would be placing it where new babies have the best chance to land safely and to get away entirely before being captured. Hanging the house from a slippery wire several feet off the ground is good insurance against cats, and having low bushes nearby for hiding and perching in when the young first try their wings, shields against jays and mockingbirds.

Birds are good housekeepers and will try to keep their nests clean, so houses should be large enough for them to move about in, but not so large that they have to bring in all outdoors to fill it for nesting. A wren house can be about a 7-inch cube, or even a bit larger. Birds need air, so it isn't necessary to be an absolutely perfect carpenter! Use sturdy wood that won't collapse under the weather.

A house may be made from one 1-by-6-inch board that is 46 inches long. The pieces measure as follows: front — 6-by-7 inches; back 6-by-9 inches; two sides 6 inches wide with one

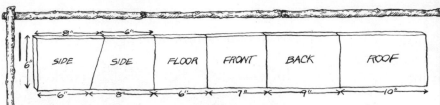

SIDE	SIDE	FLOOR	FRONT	BACK	ROOF

8" — 6" | 6" | 6" — 8" — 6" — 7" — 9" — 10"

edge 8 inches and the opposite edge 6 inches; one bottom 6-by-6 inches, and a roof 10-by-6 inches. Drill a hole, 7/8 inch wide, 4 1/2 inches from the bottom edge of the front piece and two 1/4-inch holes each in the side pieces near the top. Drill one 1/4-inch hole an inch below the 7/8-inch entrance hole and insert a 2-inch long 1/4 inch thick dowel piece. Glue in the dowel, if the fit isn't snug.

Assemble by nailing the front and back pieces to the sides, leaving 1 inch below the length of the sides. Place the bottom piece between these extensions flat across the bottom edges of the pieces. Nail the bottom to the sides and ends.

Nail the sides to the roof leaving an overhang at the back and front. Screw the screw eye into the top. There will be a little triangle of space at each side between the roof and the end pieces.

①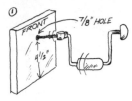

DRILL 7/8" HOLE IN FRONT AND 1/4" HOLES IN SIDES.

② DRILL 1/4" HOLE IN FRONT, 1" BELOW THE 7/8" HOLE AND INSERT 2" DOWEL.

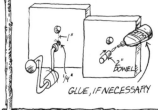

GLUE, IF NECESSARY

③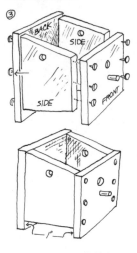

NAIL FRONT AND BACK TO SIDES. LEAVE 1" BELOW SIDES.

④

NAIL BOTTOM TO SIDES LIKE THIS —

⑤ NAIL ON ROOF, LEAVE OVERHANG AT BACK AND FRONT

⑥ SCREW IN THE SCREW EYE. HANG.

(NOTE TRIANGLES OF SPACE)

places all around. They are important hiding and fishing areas for many kinds of birds and small animals, and some, like pack rats and muskrats, live in them luxuriously. Pack rat houses get bigger every year as new apartments are built on top of the ones from last year. Other animals move into the older parts, and sometimes loons build their nests on top of the whole structure. When you poke into them, there is no end to what can be found: shiny buttons, pop-bottle lids, shoelaces. One time I found a spool of metal thread I thought I had lost forever.

In springtime and early summer, meadows are colorful with their flowers and bright, flitting birds building nests in the grass and swaying on weed stalks as they perch there to sing. Once at the lake, in the tangle of vines and berries that made the edge between marsh and meadow, the wild canaries came in a sudden migration and made me think the thicket was alive with dancing golden fairies. The variety of birds found there is one of the riches of meadow life. Of course, that is true about forests and trees, too, but the great game birds like the quail, pheasant, and grouse and the exquisite songbirds like the goldfinches and warblers choose meadows and streams and grain fields. Groups of burrowing owls can be found near dusk, turning their heads to pretend they aren't there when you come upon them.

People have always enjoyed birds being a close part of their lives; keeping them in cages and aviaries, stuffing and mounting them, and even creating imitation songbirds using music boxes for their songs. I have always had a pet canary. One of my earliest experiences with a sick pet was when my canary caught pneumonia. He was my treasure and I nursed him carefully. Nevertheless, he died as sick birds most often do. Since that time I've learned more about how to help birds when they are sick and also how to keep them well. Canary birds can live for a long time, but most birds have an extremely short life in the wild.

53

We headed for the meadows to gather flowers.

I very often find a bird that has died for some unknown reason, and I have learned how to preserve them. My first effort was the result of thinking I wanted to become a great surgeon. I found a dead owl at the foot of a huge pine tree and dissected it with a pair of crude kitchen scissors. My father was very cross and told me I had no right to do that to the owl, dead or alive. He was right. I'd only made a bad job and didn't learn anything, except that owls have more feathers than anything else. Eventually I found someone who could teach me. As with so many crafts, I discovered the main ingredients for doing a good job were patience, practice, and the proper tools.

There are two kinds of mounts for birds. One is the beautiful exhibition mount which is an imitation of the creature in real life; the other is the museum mount meant for observation and study. This is the one found in all natural history museums and good biology classes.

Beautiful Treasures

Another beauty who shows up in summertime meadows is the butterfly. Sometimes you're lucky enough to find a caterpillar making its sticky preparations for becoming a butterfly. You can visit each day and watch it change. A great day is when you see the newly hatched butterfly unfold wet wings and stand to dry in the sun. Butterflies don't have very long lives and often you can find perfect butterflies that are dead for no apparent reason. I began a collection of those a long time ago.

My cousin's father was Walter P. Taylor, a renowned naturalist, and he had taught his family some special skills and attitudes. *Collecting,* he felt, meant being orderly, selective, and purposeful; whereas *gathering* frequently resulted in taking more than you require and can lead to waste and even harm to a species. He encouraged me to take only what I needed for study or for completing and filling out a group subject, and then only if such an activity could not be accomplished without taking specimens. Many things can be learned and enjoyed right in the out-of-doors without being taken home at all. This is probably one of the best ways for all of us to be able to see and enjoy the countryside, helping to take care of it for the others who will come after us.

The number and variety of insects found in meadows are beyond imagination. Some of the most interesting are the hordes that come out to eat and live at night! A good trick for catching moths is to use a light. They will come to it, especially a hanging lantern, and if you place a bed sheet or white paper underneath the lantern, you can pick up your choice as it falls. Mounting them, especially the beautifully colored butterflies and moths, can be done so that they look like a painting. Sometimes people make whole miniature scenes using dried grass, twigs, and flowers, and then they mount their choice butterflies or moths in the scene, just as they saw them in nature.

There are many ways to save the flowers and leaves for such displays. Some flowers grow naturally so that they last without being treated at all. These belong to the everlasting family and are strawlike to touch. Others need your help to keep their color and shape. But most of these flowers can be saved perfectly with a little care. Even fluffy dandelions and thistles can be saved by delicately spraying a light lacquer or hair spray over them.

One of the oldest and most useful ways to preserve flowers is to use sand. The sand must be fine and well-worn so its grains have no sharp edges to cut the fragile flower petals. Hobby stores now sell a special packaged material called *silica gel* for this purpose, with directions for using it. Just the same, many parts of our country have perfect sand and by careful sifting and feeling, you can often find enough to use.

{ How to Make a Field I.D. Kit }

Materials needed: file cards, unlined, 5-by-7 inches; clear contact paper (hardware store); two rubber bands; mat board or rigid cardboard.

This field identification system was devised by Vincent Roth, director of the Southwest Research Station that the American Museum of Natural History maintains in Portal, Arizona. People journey from all over the world to study and do research there and this has proved to be a worthy, handy tool for beginners and professionals alike.

The kit is assembled as follows: (1) mat board, (2) approximately 50 file cards, (3) mat board, (4) rubber bands around all to keep secure and work as a press. Specimens collected are placed between cards allowing a blank card between two that enclose a specimen.

Notations can be made on the specimen card at that time or soon after finishing the collecting and identifying. Allow time for the specimen to dry thoroughly, and then cover it with clear contact paper. File the completed cards and add new clean ones to your minipress. This press may be conveniently carried in a pocket.

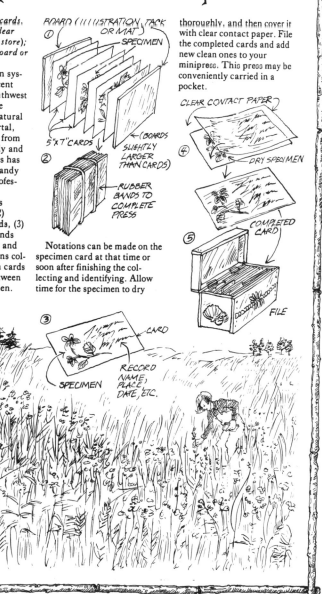

① BOARD (ILLUSTRATION, TACK OR MAT)
SPECIMEN
5"x7" CARDS
(BOARDS SLIGHTLY LARGER THAN CARDS)
② RUBBER BANDS TO COMPLETE PRESS
④ CLEAR CONTACT PAPER
DRY SPECIMEN
COMPLETED CARD
⑤ FILE
③ CARD
SPECIMEN
RECORD NAME, PLACE, DATE, ETC.

When you start doing things like saving beautiful insects and shells and flowers, you can bring your attention to the whole world of nature in a way that you may never have experienced before. This is a good way of practicing to *see*.

{Learning from the Birds}

When you learn to *see,* it isn't hard to find out what's been going on in the meadow. Snakes leave a diagonal mark in the dust, telling where they've been. Birds and mice leave scratchy looking places. Grass piled up a bit unnaturally often has a hole poked into a side of the pile that leads to a nest or a burrow. Feathers on the ground can tell us who has been there and why. Sometimes a depression means a bird will have just taken a dust bath, but if there are broken feathers, then that bird was probably some animal's dinner.

Tracks and nests are storytellers if we can *see* what we look at. Meadows have hundreds and hundreds of living places in them, and if you sit still and look closely, you'll almost lose count of the animal villages and houses you can see. Start with anthills, gopher towns, and spider and insect caves. Next count the mice nests and snake holes and badger burrows and rabbit forms and ground nests belonging to birds.

It gives me the shivers when I see dune buggies or motorcycles zipping *through* meadows and deserts instead of on designated trails. I know the drivers can't see such things as the mother kildeer running away, limping, to lead intruders away from her young in their nest. A week later that same elegant lady bird strides proudly along with her young who look like miniature striped fluff balls on toothpick legs teetering along behind her. Well, *no one* who had seen her would wreck her house, I'm sure. But her nest is just a

(*Text continued on page 62.*)

58

One time I found a spool of thread I thought was lost forever.

{How to Preserve Flowers and Leaves}

—— DRIED FLOWERS ——

Materials needed: sand, coffee can, spoon, fine watercolor brush.

Sift some sand into a box or container such as a coffee can that can be tightly closed. Place

① SAND — SIFT A LITTLE SAND INTO CAN

CLOSE-FITTING LID

your flowers on this sand so they don't touch one another, and then sift and spoon small amounts of dry sand in and around each flower until each is completely covered.

Now the hard part; seal them off with the lid and wait!

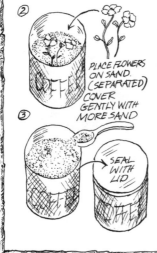

② PLACE FLOWERS ON SAND (SEPARATED) COVER GENTLY WITH MORE SAND

③ SEAL WITH LID

Sometimes it takes several days, but the silica, which is the drying part of sand, will absorb the moisture and finally your flowers will be dry and ready to use.

It's a good idea when you take them out of their sand to let them rest in the air, lying on top of the sand for a while.

④ GENTLY REMOVE SAND AND FLOWERS. LET FLOWERS REST ON SAND.

Sometimes the sand leaves a film of dust on the petals and leaves, but this can be brushed off with a *fine* watercolor brush. Be gentle so that the flowers won't break.

Cornmeal and borax are both usable materials for drying, but sand is the old standby. Great Salt Lake sand is the very best but can't be shipped or taken out of Utah anymore.

⑤ DUST OFF ANY REMAINING SAND USING A VERY FINE (TINY) WATERCOLOR BRUSH.

—— PRESSED FLOWERS ——

Materials needed: paper towels, press or heavy book, mounting paper, white glue, watercolor brush.

Another favorite way to preserve flowers is to press them and then make pictures using the dried flowers. There are two tricks in doing this. They are: (1) How to press the flowers so they keep their color and shape, and (2) How the flowers are mounted when they are dried. For the first, study the flower in nature and try to place it on the pressing paper so that when it is stiff and dry, it still looks like it's in a natural position. Remember that once it is dry, you can't tug and pull the stem or leaf into a position you'd like.

Keeping the color sometimes seems to be a matter of luck. One thing I know that makes a difference is the time in its cycle that the flower is picked. If possible, it's much better to select a blossom just as it reaches its full maturity, or better, just before, so long as you can still keep the form you want.

Press the flowers between fine, clean paper. If you don't have a press put the papers under a big book or a stack of

GLUE FLOWERS TO PAPER OR BOARD

FILL VASE WITH ONE PART GLYCERIN, 2 PARTS WATER

GLYCERIN

WATER

WATER

FINE, CLEAN PAPER

FLOWER

books. When ready to mount, use white glue thinned with water and paint it carefully on one side of your pressed flower. Use as little glue as possible and a fine brush. Handle with care and don't move the flower once you have put it in place as the glue will smear. If you feel clumsy it might be easier to pick up your flower with tweezers.

—PRESERVED LEAVES—

Materials needed: glycerin, water, jar.

Leaves alone are so different on each tree! Like flowers, some leaves dry by themselves and stay pretty. Big bouquets of several kinds together are beautiful. One way to dry them makes them turn a rich caramel color, and they last for many years. All you do is place the stems or branch just as you would in a vase, only instead of water, put them in a mixture of one part glycerin and two parts water. You can buy glycerin at a drugstore.

They should stand for about six weeks, and after that they are sturdy and don't need anything. They last long enough and are so useful that you become well acquainted with their shapes and character.

LEAVE IN LIQUID FOR 6 WEEKS

THIN WHITE GLUE WITH WATER

VERY FINE BRUSH

PAINT GLUE ON ONE SIDE OF DRIED FLOWER (HOLD WITH TWEEZERS)

simple saucer shape, open and exposed among pebbles and rocky places. It is hard to see and so easy to destroy.

Each family of birds makes its own kind of nest, but each nest, even so, is different from every other. Many birds never use the same nest again even though they may return to the same tree or bush every year. Some do return to their nests, so we don't collect those unless we're sure they've been abandoned for more than one season.

Orioles make some of my favorite nests. I just can't believe some of the extravagant oriole nests I have found. I like to imagine how nice it would be to be a baby oriole snug in such a swinging cradle. At our house now, the oriole nests are made with hair stolen from horses' tails, and they are lined with layers of sheep's wool, but I have found oriole nests made from other things. Nylon fishing line is a favorite material, and I even have one made completely of Christmas tinsel.

Once I tried making a bird nest. I had imagined that might be how people learned to weave, but it was impossible for me to do, even though I have fingers to use. All birds can do is tug and pull with their beaks. There is one thing birds do that I can do, and it really works. Most bird nests are made of some material that is woven around and around, then lined with softer stuff in the middle. If you take long strands of grass and work them into a coil of loose braid, this coil can be placed in a chicken nest and kept there for a long time, while the middle part gets changed and cleaned when necessary. Even old grass hay works well for the braided part.

Grasses are the staple material of meadows and prairies. Where there is a good supply of water, the grasses grow graceful and luxurious; they are short and stubborn where the countryside is dry. Most grass is good food and is very important to many creatures. It is also beautiful. If it is deep, the wind makes it ripple so it looks like ocean waves. Grass may have a blossom time that gives color to acres and acres.

62

{ How to Make a Grass Handle and More }

Materials needed: grass, water, cloth, string or raffia, scissors.

Grasses grow so abundantly in all parts of our country that it's difficult to believe that they exist today as a mere token of what they originally were. The destruction of the grasses which flourished on this continent is one of the sad stories in our history as inhabitants, and worse, one we are still perpetuating.

Perhaps as you search for grass to use in this project, you will be noticing grasses in a way that causes you to appreciate for the first time the natural beauty and grace and luxury of them, to say nothing of the health and life grasses provide for so many creatures, including ourselves.

Placing pretty dried grass between two pieces of wax paper (wax side toward the grass) and then pressing with a medium hot iron makes a pretty picture or decoration.

Pads for placing under hot dishes, planters, and coasters can be made, if a coil about the size of a finger is wound around in flat circles and sewn together snugly. These can be dyed pretty colors, too.

Some grasses may be cut in early summer and hung upside down to dry while still green, and others are best cut in the fall when mature. These latter are usually golden or white, like

DRY GRASS

ivory. All must be thoroughly dry before using. They may be coiled and used to make baskets in the same way pine needles are used. If used for baskets, split grass or raffia is used for sewing

SOAK GRASSES ½ HR.

COOL WATER

MOVE GRASSES TO DAMP TOWEL

or wrapping the coils. Often though, baskets and pots require handles which can be made from many materials, and grass is one which is appropriate and strong, giving a good effect. The grass handle may be wrapped or twisted or braided.

To make a braided handle, soak the grass to be used for half an hour in cool water, then remove to a towel to keep it damp for working. Arrange the grass fibers side by side. Divide the grass into three groups and tie each end off using string. Leave a short length of string on each and tie these onto a hook. Tightly braid the three hanks to the length of the desired handle plus 4 inches.

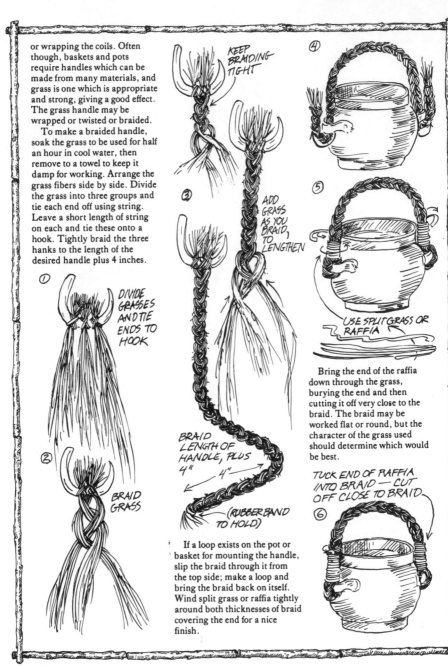

DIVIDE GRASSES AND TIE ENDS TO HOOK

BRAID GRASS

KEEP BRAIDING TIGHT

ADD GRASS AS YOU BRAID, TO LENGTHEN

BRAID LENGTH OF HANDLE, PLUS 4"   4"

(RUBBER BAND TO HOLD)

USE SPLIT GRASS OR RAFFIA

Bring the end of the raffia down through the grass, burying the end and then cutting it off very close to the braid. The braid may be worked flat or round, but the character of the grass used should determine which would be best.

TUCK END OF RAFFIA INTO BRAID — CUT OFF CLOSE TO BRAID

If a loop exists on the pot or basket for mounting the handle, slip the braid through it from the top side; make a loop and bring the braid back on itself. Wind split grass or raffia tightly around both thicknesses of braid covering the end for a nice finish.

64

There is one place near my home that sometimes looks for all the world like a lake because of the blue flowers that bloom there. Grass is also useful. It can be made into things — all the way from dolls to teapot handles to pictures!

⋅{ Red Rock Land }⋅

Meadows and prairies were formed in different ways so they have different things in them. In some places I know, meadows are made by old lakes that have become filled with soil over many years. Where I grew up, they were mostly made in places where land was cleared of trees by pioneer settlers in the early days of our country. They were also made by glaciers which scraped the land bare there. In some places the glacier dumped soil and rocks. In other places it scraped and exposed the rock. The rock in Wisconsin was usually granite or limestone. There were beautiful limestone cliffs and caves and quarries all around our countryside. The granite was equally beautiful, of many different colors, and it made fine building material.

My grandfather built granite chimneys and fireplaces in several homes. I was proud, knowing people thought they were worth driving many miles to see. One of our duties as children was to remove rocks from meadows when we came upon them, and another was to tell grandfather whenever we spotted a beautiful red rock. Red granite was considered special. To this day I cannot pass a red rock without wanting to pack it along home. The red rocks we found would be worked into a chimney or wall, and that way we learned to see how rocks could be made to fit together. Some of the best stonemasons worked in our part of Wisconsin, and their work is still there to see: perfectly cut rectangles of granite laid up in walls with the fit so flawless nothing had to be added to make them stick together.

65

{How to Make a Tassel Doll}

Materials needed: grass, string or yarn, scissors.

Grass dolls, like their cousins made from cornhusks, are made entirely from grass. They can be made like little tassels or complete with arms and legs and garments. They must be worked with dry grass which has been moistened.

A tassel doll is made by looping a hank of grass in half and tying the loop about an inch from the top as securely as possible. This tied place becomes the neck. Now carefully maneuver the grass until the loop above the tie is a complete round, and the grass hangs in an even fullness below the tie.

Trim the hank with scissors to a length of 3 inches below the tie, and then pick up two small bunches from opposite sides. Pull these out at right angles from the trimmed hank and tie them an inch from the end. Trim to ½ inch from the tie. These are the arms.

This simple little doll can be varied by using a slightly longer hank and making a tie for a waist after the arms are made. If a man is desired, simply tie the part below the waist into two parts leaving about an inch for the feet. If the amount of grass is too bulky for his legs, snip some of the excess out irregularly from the center of each section so that the mass becomes thinner, but the long, uncut pieces are on the surface.

A face may be embroidered on the top loop ball, and a string can be threaded through from under the neck tie out the top and back down through the neck and knotted, leaving a loop at the tip for hanging the doll as an ornament.

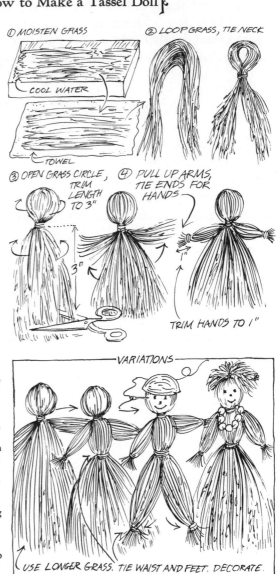

① MOISTEN GRASS

COOL WATER

TOWEL

② LOOP GRASS, TIE NECK

③ OPEN GRASS CIRCLE, TRIM LENGTH TO 3"

3"

④ PULL UP ARMS, TIE ENDS FOR HANDS

1"

TRIM HANDS TO 1"

VARIATIONS

USE LONGER GRASS. TIE WAIST AND FEET. DECORATE.

66

Our meadows and streams had many, many small rocks called cobblestones. Laid close together and flat, they were used to pave streets and walks and to make walls. But I hated them! Our town had a rivalry with a nearby town. To me and my cousins, our town seemed perfect and everything the other town did seemed a mistake. Their cobblestone street was an example. It was slippery in winter, caused unsure footing, and made my ears hurt so badly, I cried when our car rattled over the rough paving. I only learned after I was grown that the town had saved its old cobblestone street as a remembrance of a victory over mud and dust.

Inns and mills were frequently built of cobblestones and they became landmarks. My grandmother always pointed to one, so old it was going back to the earth, that her father had stayed in on his journeys to Milwaukee for supplies. It was a 45 minute journey for us when we were kids but for him, a pioneer, it had taken two days. He and his family had settled in southern Wisconsin and started a village named Westville. Now it is all gone except for a few stone foundations which show where the buildings had been.

Our breakwater at Mill Lake was made of rock, and it was so solidly built by my grandfather that our land never washed away behind it. This didn't seem as important to me as having a cement breakwater like some other people had. Ice always broke the cement and made little quiet pools where frogs and turtles grew their young. Grandfather finally relented and built another wall out into the shallow water, making a long lagoon. There we planted lilies and other pretty water plants.

Rock walls make one of the most beautiful settings for plants. The plants can be grown in little dirt pockets or against the wall itself, which makes a perfect background. Of course, the sight of a well-made rock wall stretching across a green meadow and off into the distance is probably the most elegant sight of all!

67

[The Runaway]

Then there are horses. Horses are another reason I think meadows are the best places. Horses and meadows just "go" together.

For me, one of the best days each summer was when I rode my fine standardbred horse, David, from our farm where he had spent the winter to Mill Lake where he lived in a pasture by our cottage. During the winter I used to walk or ride my bike the mile and a half to the farm to take care of David and ride him along the country roads and through the fields. When summer came, it was time to move him to Mill Lake. The best way was to ride there, and it meant an all-day trip over countryside we seldom traveled. We didn't go on the highway. Instead, we meandered on a safer but longer course through lanes where we opened and closed gates so cows wouldn't get into the corn. We rode across broad open fields and through scrub woods. We crossed pretty streams and swam small ponds. David was a good swimmer, and it must have been a treat for him to sink all the way into those cool ponds and make his way lazily to the other side. He was a calm but spirited horse, and I considered him my best friend in the world.

One summer day when David and I were well on our way to the lake, we were trotting along on a narrow gravel road and a bad thing happened. Weeds and grass along the roadside were not sprayed or mowed down like they often are today, and we were enjoying the smell of sweet clover and brushing against the blue blossoms of the chicory. We passed an especially dense stand of grass. All of a sudden we disturbed a hobo in his grassy hiding place, and he threw a sharp rock. It stung and surprised my horse. In one motion David reared onto his hind feet and reversed his direction, starting to travel at top speed. My knapsack and lunch

We meandered through lanes.

{How to Build Rock Walls}

Materials needed: rock hammer, drill or grinding chisel, wedges, rocks.

Most important is to develop a good eye for a good rock and that comes from practice. After deciding upon a project, the weight of tools you will need for the rock project must be determined. Heaving big rocks requires big tools to match. And fitting rocks together sooner or later requires some tools to break the rocks to the shapes needed. For actually working on the rocks, you will need a rock hammer, a drill or grinding chisel, and wedges. For big rocks the task of removing the rock and taking it to the wall-building site means extra planning and figuring out ways to dig the rocks up and pull them to where you want them.

Rocks very often have little hairline cracks, crevices where moss grows, or a line of another material such as quartz. Any such place is a likely one to try splitting the rock. The main reason for splitting a rock is to make a flat surface or if you suspect an unusual inside surface.

If there is no obvious place to begin a split you need, you can try making a scratch and then with even pressure tap along the length of the scratch several times. Sometimes this will cause a crack, and then you can hammer a wedge into it. If it stays stubborn, holes can be drilled in a line and then wedges put into the holes, but that is really a long, hard, hard job. Remember that when you hit a rock, even along a crevice, chips of rock may fly, so be careful of your eyes.

Laying up the rock is another job that takes practice. Whether your job is a wall or a walk, it is important to plan and make a good bed for the rocks to rest on. Besides a clean, level bed — slightly below the surrounding surface — some drainage should be provided. This can be done either by sloping the bed or by digging a separate ditch next to the bed and filling it with gravel.

Try to have a big supply of rock at hand when you build, because it often takes several tries to find a rock that just fits.

SITE FOR ROCK WALL

METHOD I

(CUT-AWAY VIEW)

PEBBLES IN DRAINAGE DITCH — LOWERED, LEVEL BED

Rock walls can be built by casually piling up rocks, usually round, into a continuous pile. Sometimes posts can be sunk at intervals and topped by rails.

Another way to work with round rock is to build two walls side by side and pour dirt, sand, or mortar between them as you raise the height of the walls.

METHOD II

The most substantial and beautiful walls are made with flat rock, sometimes cut to fit. They are laid up so that two rocks fit over one, then one over two. This gives great strength to the wall even when the ground shifts underneath from moisture or cold.

METHOD III

scattered to the far winds, and I only guessed what had happened when I heard the high cackle of a laugh as we sped by the man in the grass. When David reared, I lost my seat but, instead of being thrown clear, my foot caught in the stirrup. I was left to bounce and be dragged along by that foot. Somehow after minutes of scraping and crashing, I did manage to grab that foot and then the leather just above the stirrup. I rode all the way back to the barn hanging on for dear life to that piece of leather looking, I imagine, like a little laundry bag on the side of a horse. David didn't even stop when we came to the barn. He cantered right in and slid to a stop in his own straw-filled stall. Only then was I able to get out of that awful position, undo the girth, and let the saddle fall. My parents had always insisted I wear boots and long sleeves and pants when I rode, so even though my clothing was tattered, I was still in one piece. David's beautiful mahogany coat was covered with foam, his sides were heaving, and all I could think of was *founder,* the dread crippling that horses sometimes suffer after such an overheating. It would mean walking and walking him, preferably in a cool stream. Who could do that? My leg was so bruised that I knew I'd have to cut the boot to get it off! Finally I decided on a compromise and found a big tub that I could fill with cold water. It was painful for both of us; but I managed to soak all his legs thoroughly, and by evening I was sure he was out of danger. The farmer came in from the fields to milk, and I begged him to take me home. He did and then it was my turn to soak — in the lake.

Later my grandfather hauled David out to the lake in a stock truck, and we had good rides together. That was the summer I gained permission to ride bareback! David seemed to know things were different, and instead of teasing and playing his usual game of running off unless I had a sugar lump or corncob to offer, he came to me nuzzling and standing quietly by the fence so that I could mount easily. We

71

became better friends than ever, and when it was time to leave that summer to go *up north,* it was especially hard for me to say good-bye.

⟨Belgians and Buffalo Chaps⟩

I am sure the horses I grew up with influenced my liking for meadows and prairie land. We always had a horse around to ride. My father's father was a blacksmith, and he had a huge horse that he rode with both my brother and me perched behind him. Sometimes we rode to nearby farms where he would repair some machinery, and we would visit with the farmer's wife and play with the children. Sometimes this meant a hike out across a meadow to a stream for gathering watercress or blackberries.

My other grandfather raised purebred Belgian draft horses. They were wonderful. Our favorite was Molly. She was so ample that we cousins could all ride her at once. Her colts were famous, and we spent hours and hours teaching them to lead, wading through deep pasture grass to the far corners of their meadows just to be with them. They nuzzled and nickered and loved us. And we loved them. When fair time came, the Belgians went into the show circuit and won prizes of gold cups and colorful ribbons. Sometimes there would be too many competitions scheduled for the same hour. Then grandpa would allow one of us children to lead one horse through its paces while he showed another. We put cots in their stalls at the fairgrounds and slept there to make sure nothing happened to our animals. They trusted us and we trusted them. Just the same, we did have to learn their ways. Surprising them is one of the surest ways to get into trouble with horses, and we all had experiences learning that lesson.

One time we had a young and spirited horse that was ideal for children because he was bigger than a pony but not huge

⋅[How to Make a Bird Feeding Station]⋅

Materials needed: scrap wood and lumber, hammer, nails, saw, wooden molding, hurricane glass or juice can, birdseed.

Bird feeding stations may be anything from a clean slab of sidewalk where food is given regularly to expensive posts filled with attractively decorated structures. The Audubon Society and Ranger Rick Magazine are good sources for ideas and information about birds and their habits and requirements.

One time when my father was confined to bed with two broken legs, we consulted the Audubon Society for ideas about feeding stations and developed several successful arrangements that kept birds near the house and dad's window outlook for much of the year.

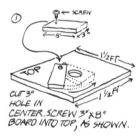

① SCREW
CUT 3" HOLE IN CENTER. SCREW 3"×8" BOARD INTO TOP, AS SHOWN.

Now, we have a meadow station, and it is the one we like best. The top and bottom are made of two 1½-foot squares. The top piece has a 3-inch hole cut out of the center and a piece of 1-by-3-inch wood cut 8 inches long is screwed into the top of the square so that it can swing to either cover the hole or be moved to the side.

The bottom square is fitted with a triangular-shaped piece

of wood across its center length. The piece is about 2 inches high and 4 inches across the triangle base and 1½ feet long.

Two sides are nailed to the base piece, the triangle piece, and the top piece. They are 10 inches long and 3 inches wide, 1 inch thick.

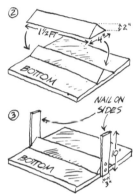

② 1½ FT 2" 4"
BOTTOM
NAIL ON SIDES
③ BOTTOM 10" 3"

Molding is nailed around the bottom piece on the top side of it so the seeds won't scatter too much, and the whole thing is screwed into the post. After many years use, we discovered that putting an extra base piece on the post was a good idea as it gave the screws more bite.

A straight-sided hurricane glass or chimney is balanced on top of the middle of the triangle

④ INSERT HURRICANE GLASS INTO HOLE
NAIL SIDE TO TOP

⑤ KEEP CLOSED OVER HOLE.
MOLDING
(EXTRA BASE PIECE ON POST)
FEEDER IS SCREWED INTO POST
CEDAR POST
METAL TO DISCOURAGE CATS OR SQUIRRELS

and its top fits in the circle top but not above it.

The worst thing that can happen with this feeder is to leave the top piece off the hole after you have filled the hurricane glass with seed. The seed not only can be ruined, but small birds go right down into the glass and sometimes can't get out. This feeder doesn't put out too much seed at one time, and it does make it available for many days.

We had a horse that decided bird seed was choice food. She discovered that she could break the glass or tip it off and have her fill. We found a juice can that worked to replace the glass, but it wasn't as handy as we couldn't see how much seed we had left. If squirrels or cats rob your feeder, a can or some sheet metal can be nailed around the post. They often can't — or won't — climb past it.

The horse was bug-eyed at the strange creature on his back.

like a full grown horse. We were all proud of his shiny black coat and dainty ways and took every opportunity to show him off. The summer we got him, my uncle came to visit from *out west,* and he brought us a present — a pair of chaps like cowboys wear. Of course they were a curiosity in Wisconsin, but such leather coverings are ideal for riding the sage and brush ranges farther west. But these chaps were not ordinary. They were made of buffalo skin, and the long curly fur had been left on them so that they were dramatic and showy. My brother was the first to try them on, and he immediately mounted our pretty black horse. It was a sight to see, but not for long! The horse was bug-eyed at the strange monster on his back and made a quick decision; he took off from a dead stop to a dead run, but the faster he ran, the more the spectacular chaps flapped and the more shouting sounded behind him. My brother's blond head was all that could be seen of him amidst the flying black mane and huge furry black chaps. He disappeared over a grassy knoll and, guessing where the little horse was headed, the rest of us hurried by a short cut as fast as we could to the Horseshoe at the marshy end of the lake. Sure enough! There they were. My brother was frozen with fright and looked like he was bolted to the saddle. The horse had apparently decided that the only way to fix his problem was to drown it, so into the water he lunged and plunged. It was no easy chore for our grownups to capture him and calm him down. And, as far as I know, they may have left those buffalo chaps at the bottom of the lake! I never saw them again.

My brother and cousins used to argue that just knowing all the life of the meadows — the birds and plants and insects — and having meadows for horses and pastures and rocks wasn't enough to make them the best place over forests and lakes. For them that may have been true. But remember I said meadows are *magic?* They really are. They have an aura, especially when the moon is full. It isn't a mist; it's a

75

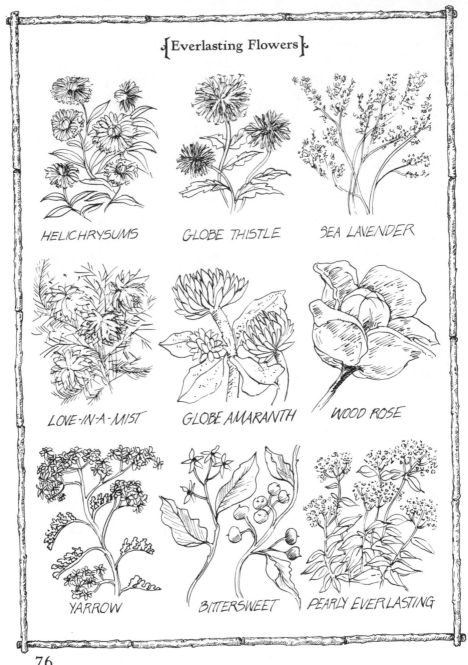

{ Everlasting Flowers }

HELICHRYSUMS

GLOBE THISTLE

SEA LAVENDER

LOVE-IN-A-MIST

GLOBE AMARANTH

WOOD ROSE

YARROW

BITTERSWEET

PEARLY EVERLASTING

76

silver stillness that makes believable all the tales you've ever heard about leprechauns, fairies, elves, and princesses. Meadows are special places for special spirits, and if you share that belief, then the life in the meadows will take you in and you can be a part of it.

I have sat still as a stone and watched while rabbits formed a circle and danced. Our black rabbit, Dunkle, left his unlatched cage to make friends with meadow jack rabbits, and I watched their ritual of welcoming this unusual visitor. He later left his cage forever to live with them. Sometimes we still see him hopping along behind a jack rabbit, looking like an undersized shadow.

We have sat at night surrounded by coyotes yapping their curiosity and howling in fun to each other. One silver night, mother fox came and paraded her family of kits for us to admire. She was proud and her glorious pelt rippled and shone in the special light. Later when the kits were older, we listened to her teaching them to hunt. She had one stationed on a nearby hill, one in a gulch, and one down the meadow lane. She barked in her rasping way and they yelped in answer. The whole meadow seemed alive with foxes! My big collie settled close to me. We both listened and watched. The magic of the silver meadow was at work.

{Part Three}

FORESTS AND TREES

Seeds, Pods, Needles, and Leaves

NE time, after I had come to live in California, my grandfather came to visit. He had grown up in Germany near the Black Forest, but he came to America when he was seventeen years old and then went straight to Wisconsin where many of his countrymen were settling. I was the first of his grandchildren to leave Wisconsin, and he came to visit me because he wanted to know in his heart that California was a good place for me. We toured the steep hills in San Francisco and admired all the famous views.

One day I decided that he really should see California's redwood trees, and we drove out to a park in Marin County. To my astonishment my sturdy grandfather wept when he saw those trees, and all the words he could say were, "This is a *real* wald." (Note: *wald* is the German word for forest.) The forests he had known in his youth in Germany were all magnificent, well-managed, and maintained. They proclaimed mystery, treasure, glory, wealth, and power to all the world. Such forests, familiar to every child who has read *Grimm's Fairy Tales* or *Hansel and Gretel,* were grandfather's idea of what a forest should be; woods that last and shelter wildlife for all time.

When we stood on the floor of that quiet redwood grove, the sun shone through the trees in thin rays and seemed a weak contrast to the huge trees. Their still and awesome strength recalled the ultimate power of trees everywhere. My mind was filled with reflections about the forests and trees I had known, just as grandfather was caught up by all of his memories.

When I was a little girl, my grandfather showed me a picture. This picture hung in the county courthouse, which was in the middle of a park. The park was in the middle of our town, and our town was in the middle of our county! The picture was taken of that same place at the time the site for the town was being selected. The town was named Elkhorn because a magnificent rack of elk's horns had been found lying right there where the picture was taken. In the picture, the only things to be seen were trees and lakes. There were eight lakes right by the town and endless trees. Now this town is busy and surrounded by magnificent prairies and farms and golf courses. The elk have disappeared. There is little fishing in the nearby lakes because it is unsafe to sit in a fishing boat while speedboats whiz by. The waters are polluted and native weeds have been removed. The wood lots on farms have gradually been changed to fields, and I find myself wondering: Don't we all still need woods and trees?

Like all plant life, trees are our living companions, but they are more than that to me. Trees and forests stand for something else; they are living witnesses to the years man has been on the earth. Just imagine the stories some trees could tell! In places where man has cooperated with the trees, life continues to flourish for him. Growing trees for fruit and cutting trees for lumber can go on for many centuries when man harvests his tree-companions carefully. My grandfather's native countryside in Germany showed that. Where man becomes greedy and thoughtless, or when he treats forests carelessly, deserts and floods have resulted. What is now

82

{How to Make Things Using Seeds and Pods}

Materials needed: seeds, pods, feathers, bones, needle, thread. Optional: beeswax, sandpaper, knife, hand drill.

We had seeds and pods of every description. Kernels of corn were some of the handiest. Grandpa grew some ornamental corn for its color, but kernels of plain, dried field corn can be strung into long bead necklaces too. If dyed a soft turquoise color, they resemble Egyptian paste-ceramic beads and can be mixed with other seeds on a nice linen string in all kinds of arrangements. All you do is thread a sturdy darning or embroidery needle with string, linen thread, monofilament, or fine wire, and poke the needle through the seed.

It's up to you what part of the seed you poke because that determines how it will hang from the thread. Generally, corn is strung through the middle, but other seeds can be effective hung from their tops, or, if they are flat, placed side by side with smaller ones in between and strung as a unit.

If the seed or kernel is too brittle and wants to break, put a few in a dish and pour boiling water over them. Leave them a few minutes until they become soft, but not until they start puffing up. Waxing the thread with beeswax makes it stronger, and it slips through seeds more easily too.

BRITTLE SEEDS   BOILING WATER

→ REMOVE BEFORE THEY PUFF UP.

BEESWAX TO MAKE THREAD STRONGER.

Feathers and bones can be added for variation or used by themselves. Bones may be cleaned by scraping with a knife and then placing them in the sun to bleach. Ant hills make a perfect place to put them, because anything you missed the ants will clean for you; so will wasps.

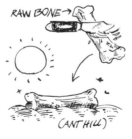

RAW BONE →

(ANT HILL)

Bones can be cut or drilled and polished with sandpaper, emery cloth, pumice, or cloth. Rubbing them with fine oil gives a finished polish and shine.

Buckskin thong makes a good combination with feathers and bones. Cut into fine strips, it can be used as thread in some projects. The Indians used sinew, which was tough and strong.

Seeds and grains and pods can be arranged into very colorful and interesting pictures simply by gluing a surface and placing the seeds on it. Tiles can be made somewhat the same way, using seeds and hobby plastic that can be baked in an oven.

83

the Sahara Desert, for example, was once a forest. In many countries rivers periodically run out of control in the winter or spring because of deforested hills.

I have thought about this country. From what I have been taught of early America, forests here once appeared unending. Even though many of our native forests have been cut, the variety of forests in our country is still astonishing. Some of the more unusual and rare stands have been saved in our national and state parks. Small patches of cactus trees, date palms, giant sequoias, bristlecone pines, redwoods, preglacial hardwoods, and even petrified forests remain for us to remember how the land once was.

I have visited many of our remaining forests, places such as the swamps in our South with stands of cypress, azaleas, and Spanish moss. I love seeing the high mountains and the timberline trees that grow in the highest mountains bent from winter snow packs, shaped and twisted by their environment. Have you seen a pine tree poke through a rock and insist upon its right to grow right there? Have you chuckled, as I have, at the stingy oak, hanging onto its leaves longer than any other trees around when fall tells of the coming winter?

Did you know that in the spring, if the ash leafs out after the oak, the summer will be wet? That if the willow leaves are cupped and gray, rain is on the way? An old-timer once told me, "The chestnut — he knows." He meant that the chestnut knew not to leaf out before all danger of frost was over. Trees in danger of drought often overproduce seeds to make sure that at least the species has a chance to survive even if they themselves die. The redwood sends out thousands of extra shoots when it is wounded.

Trees are so much a part of our lives that they are a part of our everyday language, too. We say someone is as sturdy as an oak or willowy. We say something is as easy as falling off a log. "Clearing the woods" was a phrase I knew from early childhood. Abraham Lincoln grew up and lived not too far

⊰How to Make Shakes and Posts⊱

Materials needed: froe, mallet or maul, wedge, wood (preferably cedar).

Learning to use the offerings of the woods and fields is an important lesson, not only in how to see them better, but also for making things we need and making them well. Not so long ago, nearly all boys and men knew how to split rails, fence posts, and shakes. Those log cabins that stood for so many years, abandoned in clearings by pioneer settlers, usually had fine shake roofs to protect the beams and rafters from the weather.

It takes a good eye and lots of practice to know when a tree will make good, straight-grained shakes or will split straight enough for fence posts. Cedar trees are the kind traditionally used for wooden shakes and shingles and good split fence posts.

The Chippewas used bark from the big virgin trees to build their homes and protect them from winter cold. The Potawatomis by Mill Lake used the great grasses, but with the log cabin came sod roofs and then split-wood shakes.

Shakes are made from lengths of wood which can be cut square or left round. A wedgelike blade called a *froe* is hit into the top of the piece at the width wanted for the shake. A mallet or sturdy club is used to tap the froe down the length of the wood piece, which is usually from 1½ to 2½ feet long. A tap and a twist, a tap and a twist, and the shake pops off. It is stacked to one side, and the froe put at the next space. Many pieces can be popped out of one piece of wood.

MALLET

FROE

TAP AND TWIST. REPEAT.

Splitting shakes is a little like splitting firewood. It takes practice to see the beginning of a split in a piece of wood to be made into firewood. Standing the piece on end, deciding where to land the blow of the axe, and then hitting that place cleanly, results in a satisfying *snap* and two pieces of firewood!

SUPPORT FOR WOOD TO BE SPLIT

Sometimes pieces are still too large and need to be split again; or sometimes a piece is too stubborn to split with the axe. Then a wedge is used. Stand the steel wedge in the end of the wood — in a crack if one appears. A couple of good blows on the wedge with a maul will usually break the wood open.

You may "soften" the wood for splitting by knocking it several times on the end with the maul. Soon a crack will appear. Sometimes it has to be finished with an axe.

Splitting lengths of wood for pickets is about the same as for shakes, but smaller blocks are used. Splitting wood for posts is done with the wood horizontal instead of upright; on its side rather than its end. Wedges are started in the round, spaced a little distance from one another. Usually two are enough for a fence post length. Drive first one wedge and then the other and, if necessary, finish the split with an axe or a splitting maul.

Heartwood is the best to use for posts. It can often be found in a downed tree that was burned or broken and left, so that the newest layers of wood have begun to rot away.

85

{How to Make Prints}

Materials needed: paint or block-printing ink, leaves, nutshells, buttons, potatoes, carrots, wooden frame, cotton organdy, roller or brayer, cardboard, paper.

Leaves and pods can make beautiful designs. At Christmas I make my own wrapping paper, sometimes drawing scenes on tissue, but often mass-producing designs.

There are many things that can be used for printing repeat designs, such as buttons, or patterns cut in potatoes or carrots. Nutshells are a favorite and can be filed down smoothly, inked, and printed to make interesting designs. Walnut or hickory nuts are good.

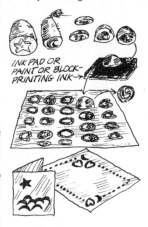

INK PAD OR PAINT OR BLOCK-PRINTING INK →

Another way to make repeat designs is to arrange several leaves or seeds across the paper or cloth; then spatter tempera paint or block-printing ink over the leaves with a toothbrush which has been dipped in ink or paint and then brushed with a finger causing a spatter.

SPATTER PAINT WITH TOOTH-BRUSH

A roller, or brayer, can be inked and rolled over the leaves, or a piece of screen can be placed over them and then paint brushed over that. You can also take the inked leaves and put them, ink side down, on paper and roll over them. Each gives a different kind of print.

INK

USE THE INKED LEAVES

CLEAN ROLLER

A simple screen can be made by using a frame and tacking and stretching coarse cotton organdy to it on one side. This side must make a flat surface. The screen is wet after being tacked and allowed to dry.

Now paint, about as thick as glue, can be poured into one end of the back side of the frame. The frame is placed on top of the leaf and the paper, and the paint is drawn across the screen.

For pulling the paint, a piece of cardboard may be cut to the width of the frame or a rubber squeegee can be used. Paint is squeezed through the holes and covers the paper below. Lift the screen off and then lift the leaf off the paper.

More leaves or seeds can be added after that paint dries, as can other colors. If using more than one color, start with the lightest and work toward dark.

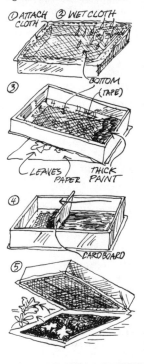

① ATTACH CLOTH ② WET CLOTH

BOTTOM (TAPE)

③

LEAVES THICK PAPER PAINT

④

CARDBOARD

⑤

from our lake country. When he was a boy, he was just like many other rail-splitters around home. The log cabins made famous in Lincoln stories were the kind of houses built in Sweden. When Swedish people came to America, they began building their native log houses here too. It was a perfect solution. Log cabins were good houses and they used trees that were being cleared from the land anyway to make way for farms. Log cabins can still be found standing all across our country. Many old ones are still being used. One of the secrets that makes them last is having a good roof. Even when they were abandoned by a farmer moving to more promising land farther west, the sturdy cabins stood for many years, if the roof was sound.

{A Log Cabin Adventure}

In my town there was an empty cabin that no one had torn down. It stood at the back of a yard next door to my grandmother's house. When we grew old enough to be Girl Scouts, I thought the girls in our troop should have a meeting place. We got together and asked her neighbors if we could use that cabin. It hadn't been used for a long time, but the owner said if we cleaned it up and cared for it, we could use it.

We were lucky because someone had built a solid wooden floor in it, so we didn't have to worry about the coldness of an earth floor in winter. We swept, washed, and polished. We put new plaster in between the logs and patched broken shingles on the roof.

Finally one day, we thought everything was perfect. Outside the front door we planted a little garden with flowers, and we had made a table and benches inside for our meetings. When it was all done, we invited our mothers to a party. It was a chilly fall day, so we decided at the last minute to make it a real christening by lighting a fire in the fireplace. After we

87

had read poems and sung our favorite songs, the big moment arrived. We lit the fire and it took off in a true scoutlike blaze. But instead of having a nice cheery fire, we suddenly found ourselves enveloped in a smoke cloud that had backed down the chimney and covered everyone and everything with black soot. Our eyes burned and itched. We coughed and choked and everyone ran outside. Soon the cloud of smoke even smothered the little fire. We looked up the chimney to find out what had gone wrong. After much poking and a lot more soot, we found the problem: an ancient, abandoned squirrel's nest was stuck up the chimney. It was so big it had blocked off the opening so that no smoke or air could draw through! We filled a gunny sack with stones, tied a rope to it, and lowered it into the chimney from the roof top. By raising and lowering and swinging it, we managed to knock the nest out along with the dirt and chimney soot. We decided after that to clean the chimney every year before building our first fire!

Next, we did a careful search of all the nooks and crannies outside the cabin and under it. Fixing up the inside hadn't been enough. We discovered that a family of skunks had lived under the house and that raccoons had enjoyed coming into the house for the winter. We located the coons' secret entrance under a pole rafter and blocked it up. We had another party when everything was finished, and by that time everyone we invited knew it was a *very special* log cabin.

{Snowballs and Robins' Eggs}

Our house in town was built out of an old horse barn. The kitchen room was added on. Where that addition jutted out, there was a huge snow apple tree. I think they are called snow apples because of the clean white flesh of the fruit under the bright red skin. Besides the apples and shade which the tree gave, it showered us with pink blossoms in a sweet blessing

88

We suddenly found ourselves enveloped in a smoke cloud.

{ How to Make a Lashed Table }

Materials needed: six poles, rope for lash (clothesline).

Cut four poles 3 feet long each. Use a diamond lashing knot (see Knots page 18) to fasten two together, making an X for each end of the table. A pole cut the length of the table is then square lashed to the top inside of the X poles, fitting the ends as closely as possible.

Another two poles 2½ feet long are cut to fit across the top of the long poles at each end. Use a square lash to join. This is the key pole. It supports the top and it keeps the table from collapsing. A top may be made of planks or a smooth-surface door or a piece of plywood.

This same X and cross pole design can also be used to construct benches and small tables.

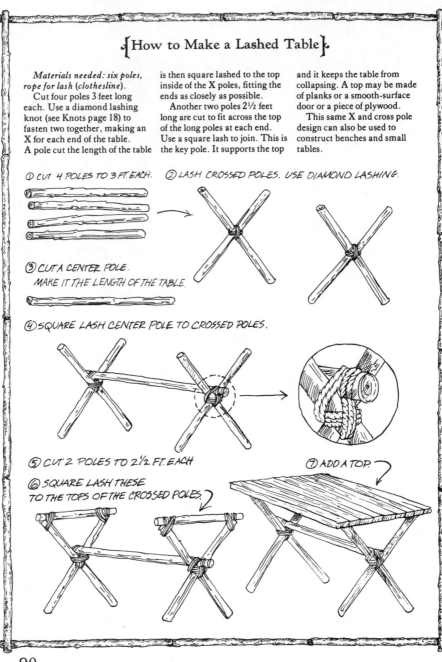

① CUT 4 POLES TO 3 FT. EACH.

② LASH CROSSED POLES. USE DIAMOND LASHING.

③ CUT A CENTER POLE. MAKE IT THE LENGTH OF THE TABLE.

④ SQUARE LASH CENTER POLE TO CROSSED POLES.

⑤ CUT 2 POLES TO 2½ FT. EACH

⑥ SQUARE LASH THESE TO THE TOPS OF THE CROSSED POLES.

⑦ ADD A TOP.

every spring. Each year at that time my father would move my big wooden doll house outside under the tree and hang out swings on our favorite branches.

In winter we used the apple tree for a lookout station. It was a perfect tree for climbing. Nearby, we had a snow fort in our yard, which we made solid by carefully pouring water over the walls on the coldest nights so they would freeze. There were similar forts in the yard next door and in several others all along the path to our school. Going to school on those winter days was high adventure, and our apple tree was an important post along the route.

Sometimes bully boys would make iceballs instead of snowballs or put a rock inside a snowball. Then there was a big fight that would have made everybody late for school except for one thing. The man in charge of ringing the school bell rang it from inside a tower and from up there he could see almost the whole town. On the days that we were delayed, he just kept ringing the bell a few more times. He had grown up using the same path to the same school, and he knew exactly what was happening.

The other tree by our house grew next to my bedroom window. It was a maple. A robin family came to nest there every year and as long as we lived there, I could count on seeing those blue eggs in the spring nest. That tree was part of a long row of maples that grew along the main road through town. In the fall the maple trees drop beautifully colored leaves, and we would make mounds of them that were many times taller than we were. Then we jumped into the mounds and played and got buried and lost in the weightless mass of color.

In summer, when we moved to grandfather's cottage at Mill Lake, we would awaken each morning to the drilling of red-headed woodpeckers on the trees. Sometimes their tapping made a roar on the metal downspouts, but most often it was a brrrruuum as holes were bored in a hardwood tree

91

The squirrels performed daring feats of leaping from tree to tree.

where they stored what seemed like millions of acorns. My grandfather often left hickory trees standing when they died. They seldom fell and when they became hollow, they provided homes from top to bottom. Small animals, such as raccoons, lived in the bottom, and birds, like flickers, woodpeckers, owls, and wood ducks, lived in the higher hollows. Birds like to have dead trees, called snags, to light upon. They provide a clear place to watch from.

I was taught by my family to care for our trees and to manage them so that there would always be lots of trees. Like so many people in Wisconsin, our family had farms, and every farm needed a wood lot. This was not only because we used wood for cook stoves, heaters, fence posts, and rails; it was also because of the other life that the trees supported. Rabbits, grouse, pheasant, and quail all needed the trees too. Owls hunted rodents, and squirrels buried their acorns, so we didn't have to plant any.

How we loved to watch squirrel games in the big old oaks and maples. The squirrels were very good at their own versions of tag and hide and seek. Daring feats of leaping from tree to tree and fast scrambles up and down and in and out were all part of the action. They were great beggars and robbers, too. They teased us and we teased them back. I remember one big gray squirrel who used to come to us for handouts of walnuts. A whole tree of walnuts was nearby, but he liked the fun of coming to us. Once we gave him a lemon instead of a walnut. He sneaked it away and sat down to eat it, picking it up in his front paws as he prepared for a big dinner. We watched him take a bite, pause, and then with all his strength and both paws, throw the lemon as far as he could and run away, scolding us at the top of his voice. All the while we shrieked with laughter.

Trees for windbreaks are another important feature of that area. Sometimes they are called shelter belts. The main idea is to give protection from the prairie winds which in winter

93

cause giant snowdrifts, and in summer make topsoil blow off newly planted fields. The loss of good topsoil, caused first by clearing the woods and later by cultivation, is a sad part of the history of this country. In Wisconsin two additional forces acted on the land. One was the action of the prehistoric glaciers and the other was fire: prairie grass fires and forest fires.

⟨Caught in a Ring of Fire⟩

On the very same day that Mrs. O'Leary's cow started the famous Chicago Fire, there was a forest fire in Wisconsin. Because of the Chicago Fire publicity, hardly anyone has ever heard of the Peshtigo Fire, but it was the largest forest fire in history and one of the worst fires of any kind. In that sparsely settled country, there was no way to stop it, and it raged out of control, burning whole counties and making thousands of people and animals homeless.

It seems like people feared fire more in those days. One time when we were driving on our way north, we were called to a stop at the edge of a small town. We had been enjoying the drive alongside a trout stream, but when the man hailed us to stop, we knew something terrible was wrong. He asked us to help the town in a bucket brigade! Everyone who could furnish a bucket or lift one was needed. Our grownups fell into the line of people who were passing the water-filled buckets in a steady flow from the stream to a fire that had started at the edge of town. It was a sobering business, and I felt very helpless and small, just like the small forest creatures must have felt as they watched.

Another time, while we were in camp *up north,* we began to notice that the animals and birds in the forest around us seemed restless. A fawn and doe bounded straight through camp, scarcely noticing where they were. We were amazed!

94

⟨How to Make a Wooden Spoon⟩

Materials needed: a 12- to 14-inch piece of wood, jackknife, sandpaper, a gouge, wax or oil, saw.

The first thing to learn in doing any project which uses a jackknife is a respectful attitude toward your knife. If you have this attitude, then you aren't likely to injure yourself or anyone else, and your knife will always be ready to work for you. The basic care of any knife can be put into a few simple rules. I have eight stitches in my left index finger which help me to remember the rules, but it's better to learn before you hurt yourself.

(1) Choose a knife that's the right size for the job you are going to do.

(2) Keep your knife clean, honed sharp, and oiled.

(3) Use your knife as a knife. Blades are not screwdrivers or can openers, and knicks in blades cause uneven handling, which can be dangerous.

(4) Place an open knife down flat, not on its edge.

(5) To pass an open knife to another person, give the handle first.

Select a piece of wood, which is thoroughly dry, with long clear grain. It can be from the family woodpile or it can be from a lumberyard. The piece should be trimmed into a block about 12 inches long and 3 inches thick and square. Use pine or a hardwood.

Sketch the spoon shape on the length of the block; the long grain should run the length. Saw away the part of the block around what will be the handle, and roughly saw the shape of the spoon bowl.

① DRAW SPOON

② SAW ROUGH SHAPE

Using the jackknife, whittle down the piece left for the handle and shape it into the bowl. Move the knife away from you toward the bowl.

Now whittle the sides gradually to shape the bowl. Turn it upside down and shape the bottom. The gouge should be used just for the inside of the bowl. Gouges are best used along the grain of the wood (with the grain).

③ SHAPE HANDLE

④ SHAPE BOWL SIDES

⑤ SHAPE BOTTOM

Start at the handle end and, working away from you, gouge toward the center of the bowl, away from the handle. Gradually move around the bowl until it appears necessary to gouge from the tip end of the bowl. Repeat for the second half, gouging as much with the grain as possible, until a uniform thickness is achieved for the whole bowl.

⑥

USE SPOON GOUGE TO CUT INSIDE OF BOWL.

Sand the whole spoon until it feels smooth enough to use. Polish it with wax or soak it in warm vegetable oil.

⑦ SAND SMOOTH. WAX OR SOAK IN VEGETABLE OIL.

Almost any wood which is hard enough to stand wear and tear makes a good spoon. My treasure for many years was one I inherited and used many times each day. It was made of bird's-eye maple. Finally it became so thin that it simply broke in two. Often the shape of a piece of wood itself suggests the shaping of the spoon bowl and handle. Making spoons is a hobby you can enjoy all your life and one that will always give pleasure to others, too.

Finally, some friends from the Indian village came by and said they thought there was probably a fire. They were going to scout it out. Before long they returned and with them was a forest ranger. He asked us how long our supplies would last and reported that we were completely cut off from any road out of the area. The village and our camp were encircled by a forest fire! It wasn't close, but it made escape impossible.

The villagers and animals had been unable to detect the nature of the fire because it was burning in a circle, and there was no clue as to its direction. No one could judge where it was coming from or where it was going. The ranger hurried away saying he would return when he could let us know how to leave camp safely.

Well, this was one time I learned about *being ready!* The days dragged on. The sky became a sickening yellow. The skittering and chattering of the chipmunks and birds made us all nervous. I made excuses to stay in our tent. Games of cards and some books we had brought suddenly seemed very interesting. My mother and father held quiet conversations with my aunt and uncle. I know now they were solemnly making plans. If we were really trapped, the Chippewas knew how to get out by old waterways that their ancestors had used. This would be risky, but possible. The adults made two plans for the exact moment when they knew we must act. One was to leave the camp by car and the other was by boat, leaving our car and tents for the fire to burn.

At last one day my uncle's Chippewa friend came running into camp. He called, "C'mon!" and we did! We all knew our jobs and did them instantly. He told us to bring our car. Everything not absolutely necessary for everyday use had already been packed. We quickly dismantled the rest of the camp and were fleeing after the dust of his jalopy in what must have been record time.

We followed along, going on trails we had never known. Soon we came to an open road. Around us were smoldering

96

woods, charred fallen trees, and flickering fires. Blinking in the dust and smoke, our Indian friend waved us to go in a certain direction, and we went with a grateful gesture and a good-bye. The road was strewn with flaming debris. We were uncertain. After driving a few miles, we came to fire fighters who explained that there was an unexpected, temporary break in the fire due to a shift in wind and the "back" fires the Indians had started at just the right places. "Back" fires are constructed up ahead in the path of a forest fire in hopes of burning back all the fuel the original fire would have fed upon. When the original forest fire burns up to the place where the back fire was, there is no more fuel to burn and the forest fire is cut off. The Indians knew how to do this and had protected their lands for many years, but no one can make a defense against some things that people will do. We later heard that some crazy person had set that fire.

⟅Wild Creatures and Us⟆

One of the excitements in approaching our camping spot by the lake was going over narrow strips of land which connected one section of forest to another, with water in between. Whole forests, drowned by the flooding for a power station, were under that water. It was called the Chippewa Flowage, named after the Chippewa River that flowed through it. The giant dead trees had become lookout stations for herons, kingfishers, and other birds who nested near there.

One time we heard a screech and wild cries in the sky and stopped to watch a whole battle take place between an eagle and a heron. The eagle and the heron were both fishing, but the eagle had glided too far into the heron's territory. We knew where the eagle's nest was — bigger every year — but had not seen the heron's nest. It turned out to be almost

97

under the place where they were fighting, so that must have been the reason for the fight. To our surprise, the heron won and the eagle went away. The eagles had been long gone from the lake and farm areas of southern Wisconsin, as had most of the herons; so seeing them was a sure sign we really were *up north!*

Another sign was the gray wolf. We would sing around the campfire late at night, and once in a great while we could see the eyes of the wolf glowing in the light at the edge of the woods that surrounded our camp. Many animals love the sound of music and will make great efforts to listen to it. Wolves are very sociable, so it wasn't surprising to have them come. It seemed so natural that even if they howled, it wasn't frightening.

I was usually dividing my sleepy attention anyway. Our nightly campfires were a joy and a worry because of the lumpy tree toads. They loved campfires. Each night they hopped as close as they dared, sometimes landing right *in* the fire. When that happened, there would be a flurry and a scuffle to make a rescue. Sometimes there were also tears when we were too late.

Kangaroo mice came out to play at that time, too, and if we sat still or snuggled down quietly, they sometimes came and did a jig on our blankets. In silhouette against the firelight, they looked like giants.

The Chippewa boys showed us how to make slingshots and how to use them. They never used guns and didn't need to. Being on a reservation, their lives were not regulated by the game laws. Instead, they still followed their traditional practices. Small game, such as squirrels and some birds, were sources of daily food as they always had been. The boys were never without a slingshot, and they could hit a moving target with such an effortless motion that it was hard to see anything happening. We never hunted with slingshots, but we did have great contests trying to hit the bull's-eye on a target. We

98

The tree toads loved campfires.

{ How to Make Casts of Tracks }.

Materials needed: tin can, water, plaster of paris, oil, felt-tip pen.

Casting is simple to do. It is a matter of casting twice and being careful. Don't lose the track by overcasting and make sure the second cast has no place to lock onto the first.

After finding a track, mix plaster of paris in a can filled with enough water to cover the track. Always add the plaster to the water. Do not stir yet.

When no more will settle to the bottom, stir to mix. Build a small wall of mud around the cast an inch high and pour the plaster ¾ inch deep into this. It will set quickly.

If the track appears too fragile, use a thinner mix gently at first. When this begins to set, the thicker mix may be poured on top.

④ BUILD MUD WALL

1 INCH HIGH

⑤ POUR IN PLASTER MIXTURE TO 3/4 INCH.

The cast will not appear as you saw the track, so a reverse one is made. Oil your first cast well and trim off any rough edges. Make a wall or use a throwaway container and put your cast in it, face up.

⑥ WHEN DRY, LIFT OFF MOLD

⑦ OIL WELL

OIL

TRIM ROUGH EDGES

MOLD

Now cover the well-oiled cast with another layer of plaster. When this hardens, discard the wall or container and pry the two casts apart — carefully. If you've done a good job, the casts should come apart easily.

⑧ PLACE TRACK-UP IN BOX

The new cast will be the mold of what you saw. Mark on the back of this cast information about the track: where you found it, when, what the weather was like, *who* it belongs to.

⑨ POUR IN MORE PLASTER MIXTURE

⑩ WHEN DRY, SEPARATE HALVES.

FINISHED CAST

Tracks can also be "collected" by making careful drawings in a notebook along with information. As you see the same animal tracks, you become familiar with the patterns shown when the animal is running. sitting, walking, or hunting. This can be a fascinating way to learn the habits of your neighboring animals.

① FIND A TRACK YOU WANT TO CAST.

② ADD PLASTER TO WATER

PLASTER OF PARIS

WATER INSIDE

③ ONLY STIR WHEN NO MORE PLASTER WILL SETTLE TO BOTTOM.

became good enough shots to feel like we had protection for ourselves when we carried a slingshot in our pockets.

The Chippewa boys were such good shots that one day my aunt asked them if they would get a bunch of bullfrogs for us. The boys were enthusiastic and started off toward the bogs. Suddenly, one of them came back and asked my aunt why she wanted the frogs. She said, "To eat, of course." To our surprise, the boy turned slightly green, and his eyes practically popped out of his head. He said, "Well! I've *heard* of people who eat snakes and frogs, but I've never *seen* one before!" And away he ran.

The boys not only refused to bring any frogs, but they didn't come to visit for a few days, either. When they did, one of them happened to shoot a chipmunk but only wounded it. Then it was our turn to be upset. We made a box for it and nursed it until its broken leg was well. My dad explained to us all that not everybody values life in the same ways. He said that it was all right to be different from each other sometimes. Later, when the chipmunk bit me instead of the food I offered it, I didn't feel so different from the Chippewas.

I noticed, too, that when my aunt and mother were frying frog legs, and the legs hopped around in the pan like they do, the Chippewa boys doubled up laughing. Even though they never ate any, I suspect they thought it wasn't so bad after all.

⊰[Keeping Track]⊱

At home, by the lake and farm, we were familiar with such tracks as rabbit and game birds. There we could even pretty well tell whose horse had been down a dusty road by the shape of the shoe marks.

Up north the animal life was more abundant and quite different. The Chippewa boys showed us tracks and other signs of animals around us in the forest. At the time of year

101

we were there, the woods were full of hazelnuts and blueberries. These lured bears in close to our camp, and if we wanted to harvest any of the berries, we needed to be ahead of the bears. We also needed to know if we were near any bears, so we quickly learned to look for little snatches of fur caught on bushes and to identify the tracks and scats. There was certainly enough food for all. We just needed to be careful.

Each morning, on the sandy beach below our campsite, we discovered tracks showing who had come for drinks of water during the night. We learned the difference between bucks, does, fawns; between foxes and raccoons. At other sandy places we found smooth trails like miniature toboggan runs, and we learned to keep a lookout for otters playing and sliding down to the water. Tracks can tell a whole lot but you do have to learn to *see*. Each species had its own track, and each individual within the species has its own track. Tracks can be collected by making casts or drawings. These can help you to memorize which tracks belong to which animal. If you keep a careful record for long enough and state when and where each cast or drawing was made, you can learn to judge how heavy the animal was, if it was old or young, or male or female. Animals go to chosen areas for eating, for raising their young, for mating, and their trails stay fairly consistent.

Animals are tuned to many important things which people no longer pay attention to. One of these is water, and animal trails very often either lead to water or follow underground waterways. When you are tracking, sometimes you come to a place where the tracks of several different animals show up. Perhaps there is a reason more than one animal came to that place. Many animals eat the same food, but some have "rights" to help themselves first. You can try to discover who came first.

One time we tried and tried to find out who was stealing chicken eggs from us. At night we put an egg out on a wooden surface which had been sprinkled with flour. Sure enough

The otters were playing and sliding down to the water.

{ How to Make and Use Lichen Dye }

Materials needed: lichen (wolf moss), a 3-gallon enamel container, water, a cook stove.

Wolf moss is a common lichen in many parts of our country. It may be gathered at any time of the year and used fresh or dry. Place a goodly amount of lichen in an enamel container free from nicks or cracks, and cover it with water.

① LICHEN
ENAMEL POT
COVER WITH WATER

Put the pot on the stove and bring the water to a boil. Just at the boiling point, lower to a simmer and cook it for about an hour. Turn off the heat and let the lichen steep in the water overnight. The next day remove the lichen. The remaining liquid, called a *dye vat,* is now ready for use.

② BRING WATER TO A BOIL
HIGH

③ SIMMER FOR 1 HOUR
LOW 1 HR

④ TURN OFF HEAT. LET LICHEN STEEP OVERNIGHT.
OFF

⑤ NEXT DAY REMOVE LICHEN.
DYE VAT IS READY

To dye wool, moisten 1 pound of washed wool in water that is the same temperature as the water in the dye vat. Place the wool in the vat with a ratio of 1 pound of wool to 3 gallons of liquid. Simmer for an hour or more.

⑥ MOISTEN WOOL; SIMMER 1 HOUR
LOW 1 HR

Simmering the lichen and the wool gives off a strong, pungent smell. Some people object to the smell and prefer to dye out-of-doors. When the wool has taken up a yellow green color, remove the pot from the heat and let it cool thoroughly. Then rinse the wool in clean water until the water runs clear and free of color. Keep the temperatures constant and squeeze —don't wring — the wool. Hang it up to dry in the shade.

⑦ COOL. (WOOL STILL IN POT)

⑧ REMOVE WOOL. RINSE

RINSE UNTIL WATER IS COLOR-FREE.
⑨ HANG IN SHADE TO DRY.

Lichen contains its own mordant. *Mordant* is a Greek word meaning "to bite." A mordant causes the color to bite or fix into the fiber, so it won't wash out or run. But lichen can be made to last in its sunny brightness for many more years by using wool mordanted with alum. To do this, add 1 pound of washed wool to a mixture of 4 ounces of potassium alum (buy at a drugstore) and 3 gallons of water. Simmer for one hour, cool, and rinse.

there were tracks each morning, but for some reason they were always blurred. Finally one day, there were clear, distinct mouse tracks. Since mice don't eat eggs, they must have come for a sample of the flour! The next night I left the egg, but I put white chalk dust under and around it. In the morning perfect fox prints were there in the dust.

Foxes love eggs. Some people even call them egg-suckers. They puncture a small hole in an egg with their teeth and draw the contents out by sucking it. If you have ever tried to empty an egg by blowing it so that you can keep the shell, you can imagine what a neat trick this is for a fox.

{Colors from Plants}

Lichen is one of the foods many animals of the forest eat. It is one of the all-purpose plants of the forest. In fact, lichen and its close relative, moss, are found just about everywhere. They are both used for food and as nesting material by animals. People use them for a variety of things, too. Most lichens appear to be dull and unattractive, but when they are wet by rain, they can become brilliant and catch sunlight in strange, glowing colors. They look fragile, but they are tough. Often they are a clue to woodland activity. You can tell when deer have been rubbing their antlers by looking at the moss and lichen on trees. When the plants deer usually brouse on are scarce, you will see the lichen cropped off quite high where the deer have reached up to eat it.

There is an old saying that one can tell the direction of north in the woods by which side of a tree the moss grows on. The idea is that moss grows best on the shady side of a tree which is usually the side away from the sun. That is most often the north side.

Mosses and lichens are some of the most beautiful and intricate forms in nature. Some grow so slowly that it should

105

be considered a crime to even touch them, but others reproduce rapidly. Some live on rocks, some on trees, and some in water — like sphagnum moss. Long ago these plants were cultivated and prized as a source of color. Until we invented artificial food coloring, lichens were one of the few sources of color that was safe to use in food.

Colors made from plants or chemicals are called dyes. Natural dyes are made only from things in nature; chemical dyes are man-made. Chemical dyes are usually very brilliant and colorfast, that is, they don't fade or run. Natural dyes are rich and subtle. Probably the most appealing characteristic of natural dyes is the way they blend together harmoniously.

The Indians in America knew of certain plants and other natural color sources; one of them is lichen. Because lichen also contains the one thing needed to make its color stay fixed, it is one of the easiest to use.

One time when I was doing some studies on natural dyes, an Indian lady told me about a cousin of hers who, she said, "knew color." She promised to arrange a meeting between us. Many months later the telephone rang and it was the lady. She said, "You can come now." I knew that her father had died that week, so I didn't ask any questions, thinking she needed some kind of help.

When I arrived at her home there were large numbers of sad, solemn-faced people gathered about. I was ushered through the house to a remote corner where I waited by myself. After a time a young man came in and shyly introduced himself as her cousin. He said he had recognized me by my sweater made of handmade wool, colored with natural dyes. He also told me many interesting things about color plants. He was a professor of Indian culture, and I found out from him that Indians traditionally protect certain areas where plants for producing colors grow especially well.

In our hurry to build more highways and houses, we have covered over almost all of those places. When I met my

⊰How to Make a Pine Needle Basket⊱

Materials needed: pine needles, number 18 or 20 tapestry needle, heavy cotton or linen thread, scissors, knife.

The "eye" or the beginning of the bottom will strongly determine the firmness of a basket. Other factors such as the quality of the pine needles; the binding cord, grass, or thread will affect the basket too. But the Indians say that the eye of the ninth basket reveals the soul of the maker!

Essentially the basket is a series of pine needles coiled and sewn together. Select long, dry needles. The best gathering time is in the spring. They should not be old and brittle or have begun to show spots of decay. Moisten the approximate amount you need to use at one time in warm water. When thoroughly dampened, put them on an old towel to be kept moist while you work.

① *DAMPEN PINE NEEDLES*

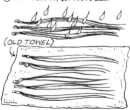

(OLD TOWEL)

A large handful will be enough for practicing eyes. It is said never to start a basket until three eyes have been made. To make a perfect eye may take many tries.

Thread a strong, large-eyed, blunt-nosed, short tapestry needle, preferably number 18 or 20. Use heavy-duty cotton or linen thread. Cut 3 yards, thread it, fold it in half, and knot the end.

Take three *shanks* of pine needles (nine needles) and lay them over the palm of your left hand with the stubs lined up across your index finger. Lay the thread alongside of the pine needles with the knot hanging an inch longer than the pine needle stubs, away from you, along the left side of the pine needles.

Loop the thread around your palm and the back of your hand, bringing it across below the knot. Hold all in place with your left thumb. The thread is then whipped on (tightly wrapped around) the pine needles. This pulls the needles together.

② *KNOT · NEEDLE DOUBLED THREAD · 3 SHANKS PINE NEEDLES*

③ *WRAP TIGHTLY 3 TIMES*

Take your fingers out of the loop after the first few winds have secured the pine needles. Drop your needle and thread down through the loop. Pull the

knot end at the top until the loop disappears. Snip off the knot end close to the stubs. Whip around the pine needles for about an inch.

④ *PULL KNOT END*

⑤ *1"*

The wound part is now bent around to become a flat circle shape. The stub end of the shanks cross the end of the wound pine needles where the needle and thread are dangling. Take the needles and wind the thread around the place where the shanks and the stubs cross to hold the circle shape firm. Do this three times making it tight but not too tight.

107

⑥

WRAP THREAD 3 TIMES AROUND FIRST COIL AND ENDS.

The pine needles are then coiled again around the wound coil and are fastened to it by placing the threaded needle under three of the wound threads, pulling needle and thread through, and then around the pine needle coil, then under and through three more wound threads and around the coil again. This is continued until the second coil is bound to the first.

⑧ CUT OFF STUBS

⑨ HIT EYE ONCE

The third coil is added by bending the needles around the second coil and sewing them on. The needle is poked in between a couple of pine needles in the second coil close to and behind a stitch in the second coil. (Take care not to pierce a pine needle.) Then wrap the needle and thread around the third coil and drop the needle through the thread loop formed and pull tight. This is a basket or blanket stitch and is used from now on.

You will run out of pine needles and thread as you progress. To add needles, slip them in a few at a time, staggering the ends so they don't make a blunt lump.

When new thread is needed, the new knot is buried in the coil and the needle pulled through and forward to the position of the next stitch. The basket is continued in a flat disk until the size is reached that you want for a bottom. To start up the sides, gradually work the coils to a position of being one on top of the other rather than side by side; the stitching is the same. The coils should appear smooth on all surfaces.

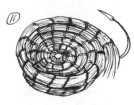

⑪

As you work your stitches, they will seem to make a spiral pattern as you progress outward from the eye — if you work evenly. Usually the widest separation between the rows of stitches is no more than 1 inch.

A simple finish for the top edge is a basket stitch around the top coil. The pine needle ends on the top coil are cut in a staggered way so that the coil ends smoothly and without a blunt end. The basket is moist, and as it dries, it will loosen so it is important to work snugly.

⑦

THREAD NEEDLE UNDER 3 WOUND THREADS.

THEN AROUND SECOND COIL

REPEAT FOR ALL OF COIL.

Cut off the stubs or pitch ends with a sharp knife. Now, place the eye on the floor and with a walnut or thread spool hit it soundly — once. This completes the eye.

⑩ NEEDLE THROUGH PART OF COIL 2 —

AROUND COIL 3 —

THROUGH LOOP —

PULL TIGHT.

REPEAT

⑫

friend's cousin, he was working hard with the government to safeguard those that were left. He said that Indians only take plants after giving a prayer of thanks and asking for renewal. He tried to persuade me not to print my dye recipes for fear that printing them would encourage people who have no tradition of caring and love to take too many plants.

This conversation made me think about more than color. My brother, cousins, and I had grown up turning to the woods, streams, meadows, and lakes as places to learn, to enjoy, and as sources of materials for our needs. I feel that learning to intelligently use the natural materials found in the woods and fields is important, not only in how to see them better and to appreciate them, but to make the things we need or want and to make them well.

As people came across our country "clearing the woods," they learned to make many everyday tools and necessities out of that wood. They made such things as rakes, shovels, hinges, latches, locks, nails, and wheelbarrows. They made boxes, bins, plates, spoons, baskets, handles, and furniture of all descriptions. People learned how to use the seeds, pods, fruits, and leaves of plants and trees — and preserving them — enjoying them for their beauty, as well.

At Mill Lake we made small pillows stuffed with pine needles. The pillows always smelled fresh and clean. We thought acorns, pine cones, and seeds were endlessly fascinating and sometimes, especially on rainy days, we made things from them.

The No-Peace Pipe

One time we cousins decided to make some peace pipes. We carefully hollowed out the biggest acorns we could find, made a hole in the side of each one, and put a length of straw into that. Since no one in any of our families smoked, we had

109

no firsthand knowledge of what a real pipe should be like, but you could blow air in and out of these and that seemed just right. We always had a working theory that somebody had invented everything that was made, so that we could become inventors too, even if we didn't have a plan.

When we got the acorns dry and clean, we ground up the acorn filling and stuffed it back into the acorn. Then we were ready to smoke the peace pipes. We all piled into one big hammock, facing in the direction away from the cottage, and solemnly lit our pipes. We drew deep drafts of air through the filling to get it lit and, by concentrating carefully, got them puffing in great style. It wasn't long before the gleeful swinging of the hammock slowed down. Soon it was sagging and limp arms and legs could be seen hanging over the sides. After that, one by one, four little boys and one girl spilled out and rolled in agony on the ground. It wasn't just that we had all made ourselves sick and had to take medicine and be put in bed; we had also rolled into a patch of poison ivy. Our peace pipes brought no peace at all — only stomachaches and weeks of itching and scratching. Acorns aren't bad, however. They make a beautiful brown dye color, and their meal can be used for making bread.

Our native forests were mostly hardwood trees so we didn't have the variety of pine cones that are to be found in other parts of the country. Lodgepole pine and spruce furnished our cones, and we used them in combination with all kinds of seeds and pods. My favorite project was to make wreaths and swags for Christmas decorations, but we made many other things as well.

In wintertime we thought about Christmas toys and ornaments and about the birds which would come back in the spring. There was a lady in our town who came from Poland when she was a young girl, and she showed us how to hollow out eggs and decorate them with feathers and paint. There were still many people living in our town directly from the

110

{How to Make Christmas Wreaths}

Materials needed: pine cones, pods, leaves, wood or chicken wire, glue, hand drill, wire.

My favorite project for all my cones and pretty pods is to make wreaths. There is no end to the combinations of things that can be put together, and there is no end to the way they can be put together, either. Since wreaths are round and are usually hung up against a wall or door, there is a top and a backside.

A good idea is to make a plan for arranging your collected materials on the backing. It's very disappointing to have all your construction on one part and find that you don't have enough of just the right pieces to do more.

A piece of thin plywood or masonite cut to the correct size and then drilled with many fine holes all over makes a good base or backing for such a wreath.

Florists wire can be strung through those holes and around or through pods and cones — even through leaves. An arrangement for hanging the wreath should be made after drilling the holes. Usually a sturdy wire wound through the holes at the top, but not showing over it, works out well.

Other bases that can be used besides plywood are chicken wire, wire and moss, boughs twisted and tied together, and even cloth stuffed like a circular pillow. If wire is not used for mounting, glue will work, and sometimes both are used together. If using glue, a flat-surface base is important.

Work from large pieces to small pieces when mounting and from flat to lumpy for the best results. Flat glossy leaves laid overlapping and covering the base can be sewn through with the wire and are an especially pretty base covering. Pine cones sawed off like bread slices make flat, flower disks, which other, smaller things are added to.

The prettiest wreaths result from careful planning and some trial and error. Combining round and long, rough and smooth, shiny and coarse objects is a challenge, and the results are fun to see and more fun to give.

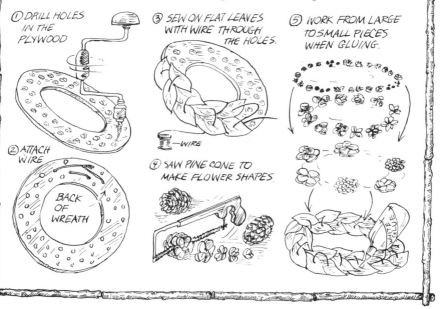

① DRILL HOLES IN THE PLYWOOD

② ATTACH WIRE

BACK OF WREATH

③ SEW ON FLAT LEAVES WITH WIRE THROUGH THE HOLES.

—WIRE

④ SAW PINE CONE TO MAKE FLOWER SHAPES.

⑤ WORK FROM LARGE TO SMALL PIECES WHEN GLUING.

WHITE GLUE

{ How to Make a Christmas Bird }

Materials needed: jackknife, wood, paint, glue, clothespin or string, and drill.

To make little birds for Christmas ornaments, we first used willow sticks and later graduated to hardwood. Pine and balsa are also easy woods for beginners to use.

Choose a stick about an inch in diameter and long enough to be held in a good grip. The bird head will be at the tip of the stick and carved first; the body will be blocked next.

Hold the stick with the left hand, pointed downward and braced against the floor. It is almost always best to move a knife with the grain of the wood and away from you, even if it's tempting not to.

Gently carve away a curve under the neck and head and another curve behind the head above the back and in front of the tail.

— CUT
CUT
CUT

Now carve another curve behind the stomach and under the tail. Your first carving will look very crude, like three ½-inch nicks in your piece of wood. Leave the body and carve the head and tail ends narrower.

① CUT OUT VERY ROUGH SHAPE.
② ROUND OUT BIRD SHAPE AND CUT OFF STICK

Carve the body of the bird to a rounded shape. When you can recognize the general shape of the bird, free it from the stick by a few cuts into the stick above the bird shape. Take the blocked-out bird into your hand.

③

REFINE SHAPE WITH SAND-PAPER

It should be about an inch thick and 2 inches long. More carving may be necessary to get a sharp outline of a beak and thin tail, but you may be able to do these just with sandpaper on such a small bird.

BIRD IS ABOUT 2" LONG

④ GLUE ON A CLOTHESPIN OR DRILL A HOLE FOR STRING OR THREAD.

PAINT

When your bird is the shape you want, you are ready to paint it any fanciful color pattern you wish for your Christmas tree. The bird can be glued to a clothespin or you can drill a small hole through his middle, bottom to top, to attach a string for hanging.

112

"old country." There was a Norwegian settlement where we went to church suppers, and they served the most wonderful food. There were Swiss dairy farmers and Swedish people who farmed or worked as lumberjacks. One silver-haired Swedish man taught us how to carve with a jackknife and how to make ornaments for Christmas trees out of wood shavings. He loved to carve little birds and to paint them in all their bright colors. He taught us to really look at the piece of wood we were carving and to think carefully about the bird. I think he loved the birds and forests as much as his own home and family.

{Part Four}

SKY ABOVE

Wind, Clouds, Stars, and Sun

EATHER is one of the great dramas of the world, and in my corner of Wisconsin, it was always a concern of everyone. We paid attention to each chance change in the daily patterns. At the lake, learning to recognize changes in the weather was as important as knowing how to swim was for us to grow up safely. Summer, when we were there, was the wet season, and the storms were necessary for growing tall Wisconsin corn. But to me those summer storms were more. I loved them — in fact, I looked forward to them and relished them. Rainy days were cozy with fireplace fires, marshmallow roasts, card games, and time for the piano, mandolin, ukulele, and banjos.

Full-blown electrical storms were much more than just rain. They meant no electricity. They meant no telephone. They meant running and racing to secure boats so they wouldn't be battered, to turn the canoe upside down in the grass, to bring in the porch pillows, and to close windows. The great screened porches upstairs and down had huge canvas shades that could be lowered as protection from storms, and it was always an exercise in speedy coordination to get them lowered and secured ahead of the hardest wind

We watched the lightning dance around the lake.

and rain. One time when I was still too small, I was assigned one whole canvas by myself. It was huge, and the wind blew so hard that I went sailing almost to the ceiling as I tried to control it.

If the storm was at night, it meant going to bed by candlelight. How scary it was to get to the first landing of the stairs. The great stuffed deer head there seemed even more huge. As the candle flickered, his shadow moved and his glass eyes seemed real. If there was a clap of thunder at that minute, it was a real temptation to become a sissy then and there! There were no ceilings upstairs so the storm's lashings were all the more resounding on the roof.

We cousins would watch wide-eyed as the lightning danced around the lake, sometimes splitting a tree, sometimes striking a boat, but mostly tearing monumental clouds in two with its zigzag of flame lighting the whole sky. We knew what it could do. We had a horse whose hindquarters had been cleaved by lightning and an aunt whose heel was burned off by it. I have stood in the kitchen and seen it dance in a complete circle around the room while I was watching from the center of the floor. It is so mysterious, so powerful, so free that more than fear I was, and still am, inspired to awe.

Our weather in Wisconsin was dramatic in other ways too. The summer my cousin came from Texas was the first year I knew about tornadoes. Until then they were only something I had read about in school books. But patterns change and that summer produced a real tornado. None of us felt just right that day, and our uneasiness grew as the sky became yellow and the birds stopped singing. It became so quiet that when my aunt said we should fix the canvas, the sound of her voice was earsplitting. It also seemed unthinkable. There was no wind — no leaf or grass stirred. Why prepare for a storm? Suddenly things happened! Just as we turned to shut the windows against the beating from possible wind and rain, one by one the panes of glass tumbled out and onto the grass outside. The air pressure inside the house had become greater than that out-of-doors! Wind began to rage, but we weren't allowed to go batten down the boats. Trees were yanked out of the ground as if by a huge, invisible hand, and many things were destroyed. We discovered after it passed that it had come in a path leaving behind a ravaged and destroyed countryside. Fortunately we had been on the very outside edge of the tornado.

⟨Danger on the Ice⟩

Nothing was ever insignificant about the weather. From my earliest memory, I knew we were all its puppets, especially out-of-doors. As we cousins grew, our grownups carefully taught us, and we learned from experience. Life on the lake had its own rules and the weather ruled over most of them. Our round-bottomed rowboat and canoe were as dangerous as hot-blooded horses. Being out too far on a windy day had temptations, though. It was hard to manage rowing and paddling in the deep troughs of water crested with white caps. But it was also exciting, and imagination soared with each triumph. We learned daily and grew to scorn the weekender who stayed out too long on a windy day and didn't know how to get to shore safely. We saw my mother swim to save a drowning weekend boater on two occasions, and we saw others who could not save themselves or be saved.

The winter weather was just as tyrannical as that of summer. When we went to Mill Lake during the winter, we brought little sails, ice hockey sticks, plenty of hot thermos bottles, and firewood for toasty bonfires in the snow. It was glorious to catch the wind in your sail, let it pull you on ice skates all the way across the lake and then to tack back using all your skill. My skates were figure skates, but the boys had "hard toes" for hockey, and the hockey games and skating

120

races went on for hours. When we were old enough, we learned to sail my uncle's iceboat. Iceboats are very fast and dangerous. Sometimes the sailing speed was so great, they hardly touched the ice, leaving the driver with little control, but lots of excitement.

Iceboating was even more exciting in our neighboring lake, Lake Geneva. In summer inland races, called regattas, were held on Lake Geneva. In winter as soon as the ice was thick enough, courses were marked out and the iceboat races began. As the lake ice expanded, fissures (cracks) sometimes opened up in the middle like huge rips in the ice sheath covering the lake. Naturally, these were very dangerous to skaters and boaters.

When I first learned to sail an iceboat by myself, the boat I used was a single seater and made for speed. I thought it was wonderful. I climbed in and the minute I was seated, its big sail filled with wind and away we went, boat and me, skimming on its trim runners and barely touching the ice under us. My uncle clocked the speed at better than 50 miles per hour as I sped past him. Suddenly I approached open water. How had I come across so much lake so fast! I stretched for more control of the halyards, and as I did, my hood blew off, my coat unbuttoned, and my scarf blew right across my face. I couldn't see a thing with the scarf plastered across my eyes. All I could do was feel! Somehow managing to keep the sail full of wind, I hauled and hauled until the racer was up on one runner but coming around and pointed toward home in a sharp tack. Whew!

The woolly scarf was snatched away to the winds, and I gradually maneuvered back to my uncles and cousins who were waiting turns. It was ten degrees below zero, but I was so excited I felt no cold. That night was the last I remembered for a long time. I woke up coughing and miserable, and my blankets and pajamas were wringing wet. I was sure my head was breaking into a million pieces at least. Mother gave me

121

hot lemonade and tried to comfort me, but when I was next aware of her, it was many days later. She told me I had pneumonia and was not to try to get up. How could I get up with the whole weight of the world on my chest? To this day I still cough all the way down to my boots when winter comes. I don't complain though, because I can still see that open water in my mind's eye, and I know exactly how lucky I am.

Iceboating and skating weren't the only things going on at the lake. Fishing for ciscos was one of the special features of winter. It required planning and a good knowledge of the lake too. Little shacks were built and hauled out to spots where fishermen thought there might be fish under the ice. Inside the floorless shack, a couple of holes were punched through the ice, and chairs and stools were installed for fishermen to perch on. Sometimes small pails containing coal fires or kerosene burners were added on especially cold days. Ciscos are meaty white fish much like a trout. They like pure cold water and are hard to catch in summer because they stay down too deep. Naturally, it's always a game between fish and fisherman to find which lure will make the catch.

One time when I was still too young to go ice fishing, my uncle came to our house. He was out of breath and his errand seemed urgent. It seemed that cisco fish were biting, and he had no yellow beads which were the successful lure of the day. My mother rummaged through her button box and sewing supplies to see if she had any to give him. Then she remembered that I had a pretty bracelet made of, wouldn't you know, yellow beads. And they were just the right size to string above a fishhook. Without a backward look, my uncle took them, flung himself out the door, and clatter-trapped down the road to the lake in his old fishing car. Of course promises were made about returning the beads, but promises sometimes have a way of being forgotten. In all my growing-up days, I can't remember wanting to have or even to wear *any* bracelet, much less a gaudy yellow one. Just the

122

Suddenly I approached open water.

same, it was mine and those old fish should have chosen some other color — red for instance.

For me the ice was like lightning; it had power and mystery. It roared and clapped like thunder. It, too, was dangerous and fascinating. The birds and animals seemed to know the exact moment when the ice on the lake would first freeze, and they were almost never trapped and frozen into it. Once in a while we would rescue a duck or goose that had lingered too long, but at our end of the lake there often remained an open place in the ice before the final freeze. Ducks and geese would gather there during their late fall visits to nearby grain fields, and it was a magnificent sight to see the leaders signal "time to go." Sometimes it took a whole day for them to get organized and such a noise they made! The birds would circle until the last group had taken off and usually the lake froze that very same night.

As winter progressed and the ice expanded, it pushed and pushed against the breakwaters, and by spring the pileup of ice became gigantic. In shallower lakes, very thick ice threatens the fish; but mostly fish seem to know — just as birds do — what's coming and what to do. In spring and fall the water in lakes "turns over." The top and bottom water changes place when the top water becomes cold and heavy. For a while when it's turning, the waters mix up completely, and that is some of the best fishing time in deep lakes. There is a saying:

> *When the wind is from the north,*
> *fisherman don't set forth;*
> *Wind from the east, fish bite the least;*
> *Wind from the west, fish bite best;*
> *But wind from the south* blows *the bait*
> *in fishes' mouths!*

Since rainstorms and winds in our hemisphere tend to come from the southeast, it seems that fish know that the low

124

pressures that accompany stormy weather are good times for feeding! It has always been surprising to me to find that people know so much less than fish and birds do!

⋅[Riding the Wind]⋅

The winds can tell us many stories, but we need to *see* them and hear them. We have a family of red-tailed hawks that live in the woods nearby. Each year one of the great pleasures of spring is to see the squawking, squeaking, screeching baby hawks as they learn to fly. First we see them being led from their nest to perch on a nearby snag and then back to their nest. Next, they sail. Their nest tree is on a little ridge, and their mother leads them flying toward the creek. It's all downward gliding, so it's pretty easy. Once they get to the creek, mother redtail shows them a place where the air is always moving upward. When their glide down is accurate, they can catch the updraft and gain enough altitude to sail back to their nest. Nearly always one of the baby birds misses the return flight while its brothers and sisters sail safely, if clumsily, back to their landing.

It's a noisy, wearing day for mother redtail, but each year it's the same. How does she know that wind is there? We can only guess. Looking at the situation, I can only add up three possible factors. Can you guess what they are?

The first is that there is always movement of air between masses of land and water. Second, the nest is on a ridge, so air would be moving up or down or around it. Finally woods would heat the air around them to different temperatures than rocks and water so that would cause air to move too. If all of these movements came together, maybe they go up, and mother redtail has discovered that they do!

The sound of the wind is another important storyteller. Sometimes it makes hollow noises and sometimes just secret,

125

{Kinds of Clouds}

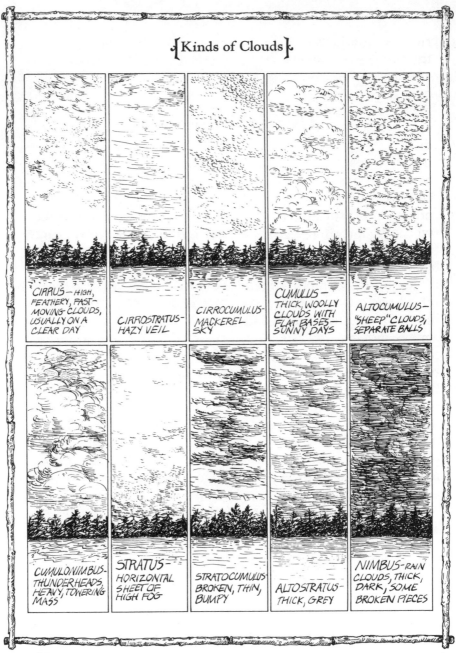

CIRRUS — HIGH, FEATHERY, FAST-MOVING CLOUDS, USUALLY ON A CLEAR DAY

CIRROSTRATUS — HAZY VEIL

CIRROCUMULUS — MACKEREL SKY

CUMULUS — THICK, WOOLLY CLOUDS WITH FLAT BASES — SUNNY DAYS

ALTOCUMULUS — "SHEEP" CLOUDS, SEPARATE BALLS

CUMULONIMBUS — THUNDERHEADS, HEAVY, TOWERING MASS

STRATUS — HORIZONTAL SHEET OF HIGH FOG

STRATOCUMULUS — BROKEN, THIN, BUMPY

ALTOSTRATUS — THICK, GREY

NIMBUS — RAIN CLOUDS, THICK, DARK, SOME BROKEN PIECES

rustling noises. We all pay attention if it howls and rages, but the sounds we hear every day differ, too, according to the air and how it's moving. Usually if a train whistle or horn sounds hollow, it is a sign of possible rain, and the air *is* hollow with little pressure. On those days you may notice that everything sounds close and loud: traffic near your house, voices a distance away, especially over water. On noisy days people become cross and nervous. The air is low and it's quite likely to storm on those days. The nervous rustling of leaves, the riffles across the lake surface, the switching of breezes from north to east to south and back again to southeast, all of these whispers and changes tell. A door bangs suddenly, a curtain billows into the room, a porch lamp creaks on its hinges. It's the wind, telling.

Did you know you could even look at the wind? Pick out a chimney that smokes and watch it every day. One day the smoke goes straight up. That means there is no wind, but maybe one day the smoke goes straight out at the side of the chimney. Wind — but what wind? The smoke goes along with the wind, so it's easy to discover by looking what wind it is. What if the smoke is all broken up and not going in any direction at all? That's probably a good day to look at the clouds, too. Putting the information from both of them together, you can find out what the weather story is.

Clouds can give you almost as much information as wind. Clouds are the storm signals of the sky. There are four kinds and each one has a job to do. If all goes right, the cloud you see can deliver either a storm or rain or snow or fog or bright sunshiny days. Their names are cirrus, cumulus, nimbus, and stratus. Each of them has a family and since they are important, I'll tell you their names too. Before weather was a science, people invented names for some of the clouds they knew. Some of them stayed well known, like *mare's tail* for wispy cirrus, and *mackerel* after a popular fish for the cirrocumulus. To me mackerel clouds look more like a sky full

127

of wool that hasn't been washed. It isn't hard to imagine how people began to give names to clouds.

I suppose everyone knows that people used to have weather gods that they prayed to. There is a story about a mission teacher who was trying to get his converts to stop praying to so many gods. He told them only to pray for rain when the wind was from the south! He did that to get them to believe in his own god because he knew storms always came from the south. People have prayed to sun gods all through the ages, and when you think about it, it's really hard to separate the sun from everything that has to do with us on the earth. Until we knew more about the vastness of space and the sun's place in it, the sun certainly must have seemed like a god.

One of my teachers once had us do an experiment you might like to try. It will help you to understand our delicate relationship to the sun. Our earth is like a ball and is moving through space very fast. Take a ball about the size of your fist and tie a string around it securely. Now standing in one place, start to swing that ball at the end of the string around and around your head. You will feel the ball pull harder and harder against the string end you are holding. You are like the sun in relation to that ball which represents the earth. If the string broke or something caused it to move unevenly, the ball would fall or spin out of control. That's what would happen to us, if that miracle of pull from the sun changed. So you can see why people began to think of power even beyond the power of the sun itself.

{Sun Time, Sun Signals}

People use the power of the sun in many ways. They always have. Before the ancient scientist Archimedes invented the gears that made clocks possible, there were all sorts of other methods for telling time. The sundial is one,

{How to Make an Equatorial Sundial}

Materials needed: board for the dial surface about 12 inches by 12 inches, pencil and string or drawing compass, broom handle or spike, protractor, road maps, level.

While sundials are not the very best method for telling time, they can teach us many things — not only about time, but also about how people can use their own ability to observe and see their world. For example, in order to make a sundial, the direction of north has to be found.

Can you imagine how early man found north in the daytime without a compass? One way to do this is to measure the shadows cast by the sun. Use a level surface and draw three circles on it, one inside the other, all having the same midpoint.

At the center mount a perfectly vertical upright, such as a tall spike or a cut-off broom handle. The shadows that the vertical makes can be used to measure both noon and north.

Early on a sunny morning, mark the place where the shadow of the upright stick crosses the biggest circle. Later, on the same day, watch and mark where the shadow falls across the circle in the late afternoon. Make a straight line connecting these two points.

Repeat the same process for the next two days on the two inner circles. Do this at the same times each day. Mark the center on each of the three connecting lines and draw a line along those three center points. They will line up perfectly if the vertical is true. This line should point to north and mark noon solar time.

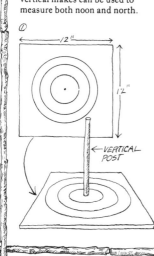

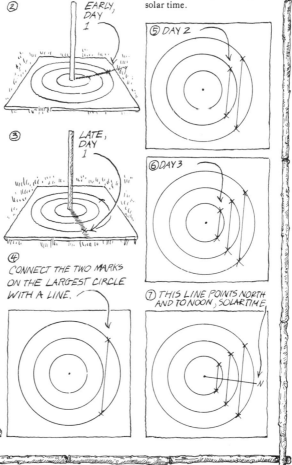

② EARLY, DAY 1

③ LATE, DAY 1

④ CONNECT THE TWO MARKS ON THE LARGEST CIRCLE WITH A LINE.

① 12" — 12" — ←VERTICAL POST

⑤ DAY 2

⑥ DAY 3

⑦ THIS LINE POINTS NORTH AND TO NOON, SOLAR TIME

With the help of a watch, you can mark similar shadow points every 15 minutes. Or you may complete your sundial by using the degrees of latitude for your location and a protractor to measure them on your dial.

The latitude is important for measuring by the sun because our earth tips a little.

The *vertical* of your dial represents the tipping angle of the earth or *axis*. The level surface the dial is on represents the *plane* of the earth's surface. As such a plane moves away from the North or South poles toward the equator that plane changes its angle in relation to the equator from parallel at the poles to perpindicular at the equator itself.

MAP OF THE COUNTRY   YOUR TOWN

If you are somewhere between the north pole and the equator, like I am, you must find out where! And that is called your angle of latitude. If you get out a road map of your area, you will find degrees (of angles) of latitude on the side edges of it, so check to see where your location is on the map, and run your finger across to the side margin and find the place that your degree of latitude is written. Subtract that degree from 90 degrees (the vertical degree the equator represents to the axis). Now, keeping the shadow of the broom handle pointing north, tilt the dial surface to that angle (or that many degrees) from horizontal and your dial will be accurate for your location.

NORTH

TILT

VERTICAL POST

SUNDIAL PLANE

N ——————————— S
ANGLE OF LATITUDE

Your finished dial face will look like this:

10 11 N 1
9   2
8   3
7   4
6   5
             6

Your whole dial will look like this:

N

Of course there are many other ways to make sundials and through the years when they were used, they became mathematical feats. The same is true of hourglasses and water clocks. The basic principles were fairly obvious to any person who could observe, but the superb and really intricate refinements people made in time pieces, especially for royalty, were amazing.

A little pocket sundial, called a journey ring, was built and can still be purchased for use today. It can only have come about because people paid attention to the sun all year, and many people made many corrections. Like the spinning wheel, the real reason we gave up the old style ways was for speed and convenience, not because the old way was not good.

Where I live in the mountains, when someone asks how many miles it is to a distant place, we are apt to answer in hours instead of miles because that is really what matters here. Sometimes, no matter how convenient our new tools are, it is good to be in touch with nature's place in our plans: in this case, range after range of mountains.

An equatorial sundial can demonstrate well how our tipping earth is in very special relation and balance with our sun. Perhaps as you learn about that relationship, you will help us all to learn how we can find even more help from the sun in the future.

USE PROTRACTOR TO FIND HOUR LINES EVERY 15°
15°   (CENTER)

130

and when I was little, nearly everyone's garden had a sundial to indicate time. Sundials only work on sunny days and during daylight, so you can see why people looked for other methods to keep track of the time. Ancient people were accustomed to the natural world around them and turned to it first for their answers. The sun's shadows, the night sky, and dripping water were all used as indicators of time for thousands of years before we turned to mechanical devices.

Besides telling time, the sun can tell you what time of year it is by its position above the horizon. As I raced to dress by the warm-air register on dark winter mornings, I used to wonder if people in China were taking sun baths in my sun. After all, that's where it went. Then I learned to watch a certain nearby roof and the position of the sun in relation to its peak and chimney. When day-by-day the sun appeared lower and lower in the sky, I started counting the days until Christmas. When the sun moved back up, higher and higher in the sky, I counted the days left of school. Soon we would move to the lake.

We learned the trick of sending signals with sunlight too. We had great times learning the Morse code. I made certain grownups pretty irritated with my tap-taps. The most important code signal was the universal one for distress, the letters SOS, which originally meant "save our ship." When you go hiking or camping, there is always the chance of becoming separated from your friends or lost and sometimes injured too. We had a certain tune we whistled when we couldn't see each other. But if you're ever really lost, it's a good idea to know how to flash an SOS.

If you have lost direction, the sun can help again. Just as it's helpful to know about the moss growing more on the north side of trees, it's also helpful to know that in the Northern Hemisphere, or anywhere in this country or Canada, the sun makes its journey through the southern part of the sky. In the morning, it starts rising in the east and in the evening it sets

131

{How to Make an SOS Signal and a Heliograph}

Materials needed: wood for stand and frame mount, frames, mirror, string, cardboard, scissors.

SOS (. . . — — — . . .) may be sent by a simple heliograph (sun helio) made by using something shiny. The idea is to cause sunlight to be reflected in a flash. The flash can even be the world famous SOS; three shorts, three longs, three shorts, if you really need help. The flash is directed toward an area where help may be attracted — even at an airplane! Other distress signals are three shots fired or three smoke fires in a row.

The heliograph has more uses. It is a way people use the sun to save their own time and energy. By constucting a simple revolving stand and mounting three frames at equal intervals, you can flash messages over great distances.

PLYWOOD SCREWED TO POST SO HELIOGRAPH CAN REVOLVE

A mirror is mounted in the first frame, and the frame is hung so that it can swing to catch the light. The second frame is bisected by string fastened at each corner which makes a cross in the middle. Then a mat with a 3-by-3-inch-square hole cut from it is also mounted in this frame. The third frame has a 2-by-2-inch hole. The three frames are mounted in a row as shown.

FRAME 1

MIRROR; MOUNTED TO TILT AND CATCH THE SUN.

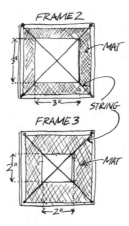

FRAME 2

MAT

3"

←—— 3" ——→

STRING

FRAME 3

2"

MAT

←— 2" —→

A tiny bit of the backing is scraped off from the center of the mirror. Look through that hole and line up the place where the strings cross with the object set to receive your flash. The mirror should be tilted to capture the sunlight, which should be reflected directly toward the object.

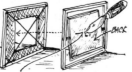

BACK

SCRATCH TINY HOLE IN CENTER OF MIRROR BACK.

If the sun is not at the best angle to be reflected from the mirror, another mirror can be used to reflect onto the first mirror. Signals can be sent by blocking the light with a piece of cardboard in front of the third frame. You block it to make short and long flashes of light.

TO MAKE FLASHES—

PASS A BOARD IN FRONT OF PIN-HOLE IN MIRROR

To mount the heliograph, we used a fallen, straight branch with a scrap of plywood screwed to the top. The branch was about as tall as my shoulder.

We could flash messages to cousins in boats on the lake. Heliographs are a great help to surveyors when they are measuring land.

in the west. In winter it's stingy and doesn't go so high east and west, but in the summer the sun stretches the days and travels in a big swing. Even so, at noon it's almost always just about south; so if you're heading north, turn your back on it, and keep your shadow in front of you.

Finding their way has always been a concern of people everywhere for as long as anyone can remember. Can you imagine yourself setting out in a little sailboat across an unknown ocean with only the sun and stars to guide you? Ancient people knew how to use the stars and the sun as guides, and we can too. The stars, like the sun, have always been there and are a part of our natural world.

At the lake we cousins used to go out at night to a nearby golf course and gather night crawlers (big worms) from the smooth, damp greens to use for fishing the next day. Because it was summer, the sky was very special and exciting. We would make bets on who would be the first to see the northern lights (aurora borealis) that year, and we would wish and wish on the many falling stars we saw.

Later one of my cousins worked summers at Yerkes Observatory near home, taking pictures of stars, and he taught me about a whole new and unbelievable world from nebulae to black holes! The myths and magic that have grown up about the night sky can't begin to compare with the reality, which is the most mysterious of all. We cousins used to have arguments about how big is big, and I'm sure the Milky Way was usually the inspiration. Who can comprehend how big the Milky Way is and then another and another? Seven hundred years ago, a man named Teng Mu said, "How unreasonable it would be to suppose that, besides the heavens and earth which we can see, there are no other heavens and no other earths." Do you agree?

Sometimes I used to lie on my back on the pier or in a boat or in the meadow on a summer night. These places were ideal for speculating about stars and for learning them. Of course,

133

the sky changes every month, but its changes are orderly and predictable. Though the whole skyful of stars wheeled and changed, the tiny North Star always stayed put. It was very pleasant to be able to look up and find it just where I expected to find it — in line with the Big Dipper pointers. From May through June we watched and loved the evening star, Venus, at Mill Lake. It set with a quiet beauty and grace, almost like a Madonna. Sometimes it was reflected in the water with its own silver path. Cold Jupiter always seemed reliably brilliant and red Mars — my star, I thought — could be easily located and distinguished from all the others. My brother assured me that there were important differences between stars and planets, but at that time it didn't matter to me. They were all assuring, stable, friendly, and part of why I liked the night.

As I continued to learn, it became even more comforting to me to realize that what could be seen is such a tiny bit of all that is out there. If the powers that were so great and important could keep everything here *and* there *and* beyond there in working order, then our job seemed to become pretty simple by comparison. Probably this gets down to figuring out how we fit in, how well we learn the laws of nature; and, at least at night, it's somehow possible to believe we can get pretty good at being a part of it all.

⟨Flying by Flashlight⟩

People have always used stars to guide them at night. Of course, finding your way has first of all to do with using good sense and all your knowledge of how things work out-of-doors; but, at night, if you can see stars, you can always find direction if you know one thing. That one bit of knowledge is how to find the small, faint, all-important North Star, Polaris. People have invented stories all through the ages about how to find this star and what it means.

Sometimes I used to lie on my back in a boat on a summer night.

The seven-star figure known to most of us today as the Big Dipper is also known as the Bear, The Great Bear, or Ursa Major; and the Little Dipper is known as Ursa Minor. These two figures travel all year long in a circle around the North Star, going all the way from right side up to upside down, always with the Big Dipper pointing to the tip of the Little Dipper's handle, which is the North Star. In our hemisphere, the North Star can be seen from any location, all the way down to the equator where it will disappear behind the earth's curve. It appears in the sky as many degrees above the horizon as you are from the equator.

When I was still a young woman in school, I learned to fly an airplane. Soon, it came time for me to learn to fly at night. The lightweight planes we flew in those early days were often ill-equipped by today's standards, and sometimes they were not maintained very well. The plane that was available to me for night flight was an old Taylor Craft. The only reason for using it was because the lights in its tail and wings actually did light up for other people to see. Most of the other planes around had no such luxuries. In order to see the instrument panel, it was necessary to carry a flashlight because there were no lights inside of the plane. The first few times I began to fly at night, I had reason to be forever grateful for all the many nights I had spent in other years memorizing the stars and being comfortable about the night. Those first few flights were on moonless, totally black nights.

For a pilot to fly without any instruments or any visible horizon is very difficult. At first I saw strange constellations and weird "falling stars." Finally by flying with my left hand and holding the flashlight with my right hand to see the instruments, I made a 360-degree circle until I could sort out the North Star, old Polaris. Knowing what time of year it was, I had a fair idea of how high Polaris was above the horizon. From that I figured out that the strange constellations below Polaris *must* be the bright lights of

towns and highways. Now when I'm in the air at night, it's a
wonder to me how I could not have known they were the
lights of towns because it seems so obvious. But then it was
the very first time I had ever been *in* the night sky, and it was
a different experience than being on the earth and looking out
at it. I was just one more of the millions of people who have
discovered what that star can mean for safe navigation.

The constancy of that little star has ever amazed people.
Great leaders have sought to identify themselves with its
character. One story about an Indian chief is worth telling
because it says so well what people of all time have felt. The
chief, Smohalla, was describing his own beautiful and
colorful flag. He explained, "This is my flag and it represents
the world. God told me to look after my people. All are my
people. There are four ways in the world, North, South,
East, and West. I have been all those ways. This is the
center. I live here. The red spot (in the flag) is my heart.
Everyone can see it. The yellow grass grows everywhere
around this place (yellow on flag). Green mountains are far
away all around the world. There is only water beyond, salt
water. The blue (a strip on the flag) is the sky, and the star is
the North Star. That star never changes; it is always in the
same place. I keep my heart on that star. I never change."

{How to Spin Raw Wool}

Materials needed: spindle, wool yarn, raw wool.

It is thought that the idea for spinning first came from people noticing how some animals and plants made fluffy balls of waste which stuck together. Some early man may have rolled a bit of this downy stuff on his thigh with the palm of his hand. Doing a lot of it made a pile, so he wrapped it on a stick.

When the stick became troublesome, a weight was added to the bottom of it. This eventually became what was known for thousands of years as a drop spindle. In many parts of the world, it is still the only spinning method used. Actually a spinning wheel is another version of this ancient technique.

You can make a drop spindle for yourself using a slender straight stick, such as a dowel, 12 inches long, and adding a weight to the bottom. A potato makes a good weight, though not very permanent. People have spun everything from gold to dog hair on drop spindles, but wool is the best for learning.

To spin wool, the dowel is strung as shown in the drawing with a piece of fuzzy yarn for the string. A hank of combed wool is held in your left hand about shoulder high and palm up.

Your fuzzy yarn end is laid on top of this wool and your thumb closes over it, holding the two together. The right hand takes the top of the dowel and gives it a twist like a top. The fuzzy yarn hangs, full length, straight down from the left hand to the dowel top.

Once the spindle is set turning, let go and with your right hand reach to the raw wool and draw some down around the string. Keep the end of the fuzzy yarn in place gently with your left thumb, but allow the wool to be pulled through about 5 inches.

Then with your right hand, spin the dowel again and tighten your left thumb on the wool and yarn to control the spinning. This pulling down is called the draft. The spinning motion of the dowel will twist up the fuzzy yarn which should be catching the wool as you pull the wool out from your hand.

When you close your thumb, you are preventing the spin from going into all the wool at once. Repeat: spin dowel, loosen clasp of left hand, pull wool, close left thumb, repeat, keeping spindle going until all your wool is spun out of your hand. It can be wound up on the dowel and your own spun yarn can be the starting fuzzy yarn for the next bit of combed wool.

RAW WOOL

WOOL YARN END

② HOLD WOOL AND YARN END IN LEFT HAND.

③ TWIST DOWEL: AS IT TURNS,

④ PULL DOWN ON WOOL

⑤ TIGHTEN LEFT THUMB. HOLD. REPEAT STEPS 2, 3, AND 4.

⑥ WHEN SPUN WOOL BECOMES TOO LONG, WIND IT ONTO SPINDLE. THEN GO BACK TO STEP 1.

SPINDLE

WOOL YARN

← (DOWEL)
← (WEIGHT)

① STRING THE SPINDLE

(RELEASE LEFT THUMB SLIGHTLY TO PULL WOOL)

138

⋈[Lore and More]⋈

THE SAYING "How can we know where we are going, if we don't know where we have been" applies to many parts of our lives. Most surely it applies to the knowledge of making useful things. Several of the projects mentioned in earlier chapters have to do with basic crafts; that is crafts that have their origins and roots in ancient times, crafts that have served mankind continuously and well with very little change.

Early people, even if they lived in large towns, were aware of the out-of-doors and their dependency on nature. In this century we are still dependent on the ways of nature, but we have also found clever ways of hiding that fact from ourselves. As we increasingly ignore nature, we begin to do something else. We behave as though nothing has ever happened before *now,* the present. Our ability to *see* our world has become so changed that we invent and reinvent things people have already and always done.

Perhaps what was a necessity at one time may now be crafted only for beauty or pleasure, and this can give a wonderful new freedom. This new freedom makes it all the more important to understand our place in the long tradition and to value what has gone before us. Understanding of old techniques can give insight. Traditional ways can also add richness and challenge to our efforts. For example, years ago I taught myself to spin wool into yarn. I taught myself because I could find no one to teach me, even though I could remember seeing Indians patiently sitting and spinning on simple stick-and-whorl spinners. At the time I wanted to learn, spinning was an art already given over to machines. It was intriguing to me to learn about the ancient Egyptians.

139

They achieved unbelievable cloth. Some of the pieces found in tombs cannot be imitated by our best machines. I was also surprised to find out that the early American settlers could spin as well as any machine. One girl in the South was recorded to have spun one pound of cotton into a thread 115 miles long. The fineness of her achievement was not considered unusual!

The reason hand spinning was given up was not because of quality. It was given up because the flying shuttle was invented, and power looms made it possible to use great quantities of yarn and so make more cloth. The days when your own sheep gave you enough wool to spin into yarn for the family clothing and blankets were over as soon as the shuttle was invented. The man who brought his loom around from one household to another throughout the year stopped coming, and wool and cotton were sent directly to the big mills.

The earliest peoples figured out how to spin and weave, to make baskets and then pottery, to use hides and preserve them as leather. They learned to hunt, first with crude clubs and rocks, and then with bows and arrows. Today we still use woven cloth, baskets, pots, and leather; and everywhere in the world the bow and arrow are used for sport, if not for hunting, and are still enjoyed. These basic crafts are as old as man. They use natural materials and require our keenest senses. These crafts can continue to give us a fresh understanding of our world and how it came to be, as well as unending pleasure in mastering them.

The directions for making grandmother's rush mat were for a simple article woven by hand. They included the two parts of everything that is woven. These two parts are called the *warp* and the *weft*. That is why some people call basketmaking *weaving,* for baskets contain the structured fiber, or warp, and the filler, or weft. However, when you become interested in weaving, you soon find that today we refer to

(*Text continued on page 144.*)

How to Make a Simple Loom

Materials needed: Popsicle sticks, wood strips, hand drill, glue, dowel or branch, thread or yarn to weave with. Optional: shuttle.

A simple beginning loom may be made for weaving such things as belts or table mats. First you must construct heddles. In this case, they will be anchored in their frame and will be rigid. A rigid heddle made of wood or plastic can be purchased, but satisfactory ones can be constructed out of narrow pieces of wood, such as Popsicle sticks.

Pierce each piece with a hole like a paper punch makes. Put the hole in exactly the same spot on each piece of wood. Make a lightweight frame of 1-by-1/8-inch (or 1-by-3/16-inch) strips of wood. Cut four pieces the width desired for the weaving you plan plus 2 inches. For example, frame pieces for a 12 inch wide weaving will be 14 inches wide. Now you are ready to glue the hole sticks to the frame. Place the two frame strips parallel and flat separated from each other by the same distance as the length of the hole sticks. Lay the sticks on top of the frame pieces, leaving a space between each Popsicle stick about the same size as the holes you cut. Make sure the tops and bottoms line up smoothly along the edges of the frame pieces and that the holes are all in a row. Glue the sticks to the frame pieces. Now glue the top frame pieces to cover the hole sticks exactly matching the position of the underneath frame so that the finished heddle frame appears the same on both sides.

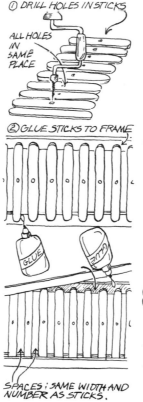

① DRILL HOLES IN STICKS

ALL HOLES IN SAME PLACE

② GLUE STICKS TO FRAME

SPACES : SAME WIDTH AND NUMBER AS STICKS.

Next measure and count the warp material. The warp runs the length of the weaving and is the base of the woven material. To measure the warp, decide how long you want your material to be and then add ½ yard to that measure. Then count the number of heddles and heddle spaces. A loom built to weave material that is 12 inches wide can have about 48 holes and spaces.

If your material is going to be a yard long, add ½ yard, giving you a length measure of 1½ yards times the 48 holes and spaces you counted earlier. But don't do any cutting, yet.

What you want now is to have one big loop of yarn that measures 3 yards around or 1½ yards if pulled tight. The loop will be made up of 24 circlings of 3 yards each in one continuous loop. Tie a string tightly around one end of this loop of warp material.

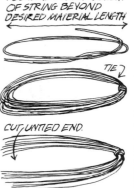

③ MAKE THE WARP.
ADD ½ YD. TO EACH LENGTH OF STRING BEYOND DESIRED MATERIAL LENGTH

TIE

CUT, UNTIED END.

Carefully cut the end of the loop that is opposite the string tie, so that you now have 48 equal lengths of yarn tied together. This is your warp. Put each warp thread through either a heddle hole or a heddle space, one after the other. It is important to fan the warp threads out and start at one side of your loom and of the warp threads and work, one-by-one, to the other side. This way your warp threads will not crisscross.

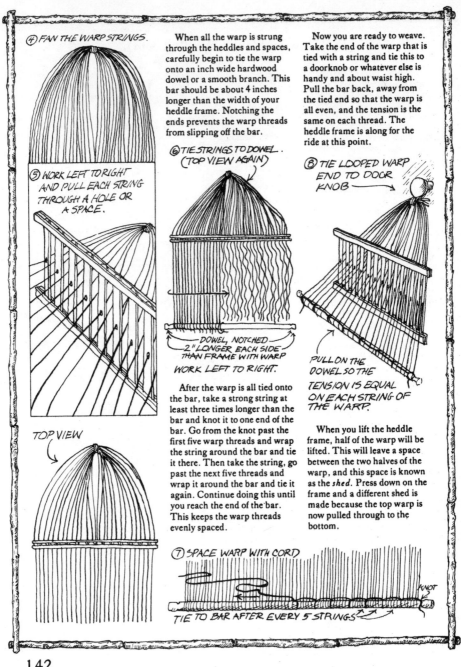

④ FAN THE WARP STRINGS.

⑤ WORK LEFT TO RIGHT AND PULL EACH STRING THROUGH A HOLE OR A SPACE.

TOP VIEW

When all the warp is strung through the heddles and spaces, carefully begin to tie the warp onto an inch wide hardwood dowel or a smooth branch. This bar should be about 4 inches longer than the width of your heddle frame. Notching the ends prevents the warp threads from slipping off the bar.

⑥ TIE STRINGS TO DOWEL. (TOP VIEW AGAIN)

DOWEL, NOTCHED, 2" LONGER EACH SIDE THAN FRAME WITH WARP

WORK LEFT TO RIGHT.

After the warp is all tied onto the bar, take a strong string at least three times longer than the bar and knot it to one end of the bar. Go from the knot past the first five warp threads and wrap the string around the bar and tie it there. Then take the string, go past the next five threads and wrap it around the bar and tie it again. Continue doing this until you reach the end of the bar. This keeps the warp threads evenly spaced.

⑦ SPACE WARP WITH CORD

TIE TO BAR AFTER EVERY 5 STRINGS

Now you are ready to weave. Take the end of the warp that is tied with a string and tie this to a doorknob or whatever else is handy and about waist high. Pull the bar back, away from the tied end so that the warp is all even, and the tension is the same on each thread. The heddle frame is along for the ride at this point.

⑧ TIE LOOPED WARP END TO DOOR KNOB

PULL ON THE DOWEL SO THE TENSION IS EQUAL ON EACH STRING OF THE WARP.

When you lift the heddle frame, half of the warp will be lifted. This will leave a space between the two halves of the warp, and this space is known as the *shed*. Press down on the frame and a different shed is made because the top warp is now pulled through to the bottom.

KNOT

142

A length of *weft* material, which is the filler or what you use to weave with, is moved through these sheds, and this is how cloth is made. Start with the frame pulled up, and put the weft in through the shed from left to right. Leave a tail of weft thread hanging down on the left side of the warp. Next press the heddle frame down creating the other shed and put the weft material through this shed from right to left.

After each up or each down move, the heddle frame is pulled gently but firmly forward forming an even line before the weft thread is put in through the next shed.

The weft thread can be wound into a small ball or onto a shuttle. This way the weft can be unwound as it is needed. Another little trick that makes this loom easier to use is to tie a sash around one end of the bar, bring it around behind your waist, and tie it onto the other end of the bar. This makes it possible to keep a good tension on the warp as you weave.

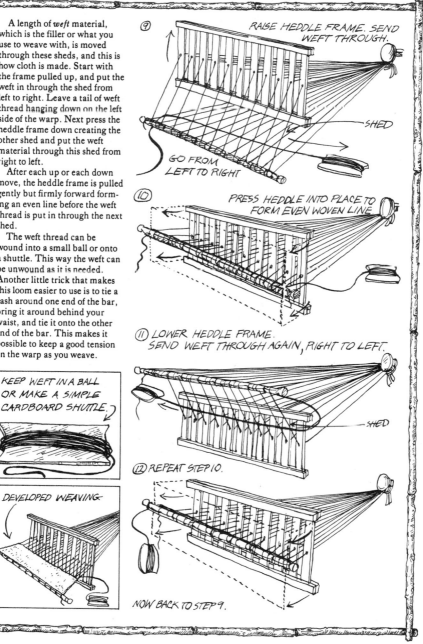

⑨ RAISE HEDDLE FRAME. SEND WEFT THROUGH.

SHED

GO FROM LEFT TO RIGHT

⑩ PRESS HEDDLE INTO PLACE TO FORM EVEN WOVEN LINE

⑪ LOWER HEDDLE FRAME. SEND WEFT THROUGH AGAIN, RIGHT TO LEFT.

SHED

⑫ REPEAT STEP 10.

NOW BACK TO STEP 9.

KEEP WEFT IN A BALL OR MAKE A SIMPLE CARDBOARD SHUTTLE.

DEVELOPED WEAVING

two kinds of weaving: on-loom and off-loom. The differences have to do with the devices that the warp is built on and how the weft is worked through it. People have been weaving for thousands of years so you can imagine that there are many, many, many ways to go about weaving something.

There are a great number of things in the outdoors to weave with. Once you start, you may never stop. Sedge grass, pine needles, strips of cedar bark, willow stocks, cattail leaves, flax leaves: the list is endless. The warp is important in providing strength for your projects. Most five-and-ten stores supply cotton-rug warp string, but any stout, strong material will do — even wire. One time I unwound a copper dish-scrubbing mitt and added it here and there in a weaving for a special effect. Your own imagination is the only limitation when you begin to weave.

⊰[Weavings of Grass, Coils of Clay]⊱

About the time primitive people were finding out that hair and fur made fuzzy streamers which could be twisted, made strong, and even spun to extend the length and twist, they were also starting to use sticks and grass to construct containers. These containers or baskets were made to use in gathering and storing food. Early people wove rushes and sticks to make coverings for floors. It can be argued that basketmaking was the mother craft of both weaving and pottery. It is also a fact that baskets have never been made successfully by machine. As Osma Tod points out in her book, *Earth Basketry,* "it still takes a good eye and nimble fingers" to construct a basket.

My feeling about basketmaking is that it combines the best pleasures of both weaving and pottery, and it is less restrictive than either one. In each basket there is the opportunity for an almost unlimited exploration of natural materials and their

How to Make Rush and Willow Baskets

Materials needed: willow, rushes, knife or scissors

Use willow which you have gathered in the spring, peeled, and allowed to dry, and now have soaked until pliable. Select pieces of the same diameter 3/16 inch to 1/4 inch. Take eight of these about 16 inches long and one a little over half that long (about 10 inches). Divide the eight into two groups of four, placing them side by side with ends even. Place one group over the other at right angles, holding both in your left hand between index finger and thumb.

DIAMETER OF WILLOWS:
3/16" TO 1/4"

10"

16"

WILLOWS PEELED DRIED, AND NOW SOAKED

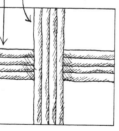

Now take a weaver which may be of smaller diameter but is cut as long as possible for you to work with; also keep the weaver the same size diameter throughout. Weave it under the four to the right and over the four on the bottom, under the four at the left, over, under, over, under, making two complete rounds.

WEAVER

(2 ROUNDS)

Then begin to separate the spokes, weaving over and under each individual spoke instead of a group of four. Be very careful and work as evenly as possible. When you have woven one row of individual spokes, you will find that using an even number of spokes makes the weaver come out the same way each time instead of alternating. This is true of all circle weaving. To alter this requires uneven warp

numbers; so insert the half spoke into your weaving, across the center and into the other side enough to secure it.

Continue to weave until the bottom is the size you want it. To make the basket turn up start pulling the weaver tighter which will bring the spokes upright. If the willow dries, dampen it with a sponge as you work.

FOR SIDES: PULL WEAVER TIGHTER

145

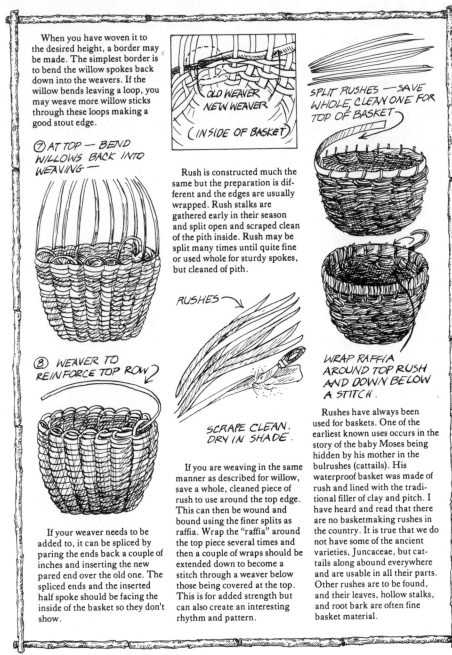

When you have woven it to the desired height, a border may be made. The simplest border is to bend the willow spokes back down into the weavers. If the willow bends leaving a loop, you may weave more willow sticks through these loops making a good stout edge.

⑦ AT TOP — BEND WILLOWS BACK INTO WEAVING —

⑧ WEAVER TO REINFORCE TOP ROW

If your weaver needs to be added to, it can be spliced by paring the ends back a couple of inches and inserting the new pared end over the old one. The spliced ends and the inserted half spoke should be facing the inside of the basket so they don't show.

OLD WEAVER
NEW WEAVER
(INSIDE OF BASKET)

Rush is constructed much the same but the preparation is different and the edges are usually wrapped. Rush stalks are gathered early in their season and split open and scraped clean of the pith inside. Rush may be split many times until quite fine or used whole for sturdy spokes, but cleaned of pith.

RUSHES

SCRAPE CLEAN. DRY IN SHADE.

If you are weaving in the same manner as described for willow, save a whole, cleaned piece of rush to use around the top edge. This can then be wound and bound using the finer splits as raffia. Wrap the "raffia" around the top piece several times and then a couple of wraps should be extended down to become a stitch through a weaver below those being covered at the top. This is for added strength but can also create an interesting rhythm and pattern.

SPLIT RUSHES — SAVE WHOLE, CLEAN ONE FOR TOP OF BASKET

WRAP RAFFIA AROUND TOP RUSH AND DOWN BELOW A STITCH.

Rushes have always been used for baskets. One of the earliest known uses occurs in the story of the baby Moses being hidden by his mother in the bulrushes (cattails). His waterproof basket was made of rush and lined with the traditional filler of clay and pitch. I have heard and read that there are no basketmaking rushes in the country. It is true that we do not have some of the ancient varieties, Juncaceae, but cattails along abound everywhere and are usable in all their parts. Other rushes are to be found, and their leaves, hollow stalks, and root bark are often fine basket material.

146

character. I have loved using natural dyes for many years, loved learning plants and the dye substances that come from them. Most of these can be used in making baskets. The Smithsonian Institute, according to Mrs. Tod, lists 103 different basket materials used by the Indians in our country. That means that just about everywhere there is some natural material suitable to use for making or coloring a basket.

Baskets have been used for more than containing and storing things. The Indians used them for many purposes, from backpacks for carrying babies to the storing of evil spirits.

One time a friend of mine who has a remarkable collection of Indian baskets was asked to the home of one of the last true and respected medicine men. The great man had just died, and his friends knew of the Indian medicine tradition of storing the evil spirits which has sickened his patients in baskets. The baskets were hidden in very old and hollow oak trees. The Indians didn't want anything to do with the spirits themselves, but they felt my friend would be safe and might like to find the baskets. This he did after some search. One huge hollow tree yielded up basket after basket, all tiny little gems, each with its own cover, and some no larger than a thimble — but all containing evil spirits! Some were so fine they looked like glass! My friend told me that one of the saddest traditions, for anyone who loves Indian baskets, is that of burning the baskets along with other worldly possessions on the funeral fires at the time a persons dies. This may be one reason that some baskets are learned about only in tales.

It's obvious how baskets and weaving are related because you can see the warp and weft construction in both. However, it isn't so clear how baskets and pottery are related. Of course, many pots and many baskets have similar shapes and similar uses too, but actually, the construction was similar to start with. Look at the coils of pine needles in a pine needle basket. Early people made the first pots by using

147

coils too, but made of clay. They built the coils inside of baskets, sometimes using only shallow baskets for support around the pot bottom and sometimes baskets for the whole pot. It is thought that a pot was first fired when a clay-lined basket was put in a fire to cook food, and the basket — easily replaced — was burned away!

Besides coiled baskets, which are sewn together and sometimes completely wrapped to hold the coil firm, there are baskets which are woven, and some are twined. As in cloth weaving, the warp material is usually stronger. In any case, it must be strong enough to support the basket. The weaver, or weft, may be the same material as the warp or entirely different. Two materials which seem to appear almost everywhere in our country are rush and willow. A basket made from either material can be as individual as you are.

‹[Arrowhead Art and Leathercraft]›

Bows and arrows are one of the most ancient and interesting crafts. Making them can lead you into all kinds of activities from searching for the perfect materials for each set of arrows and matching performance bows, to learning how to use the finest skills in constructing them, and finally to the thrill of actually putting your work to the test with a target. Besides finding out if you have made them well, you can discover how strong you are and how keen an eye you have when you score a bull's-eye.

The lore that goes along with archery is as old as man himself, for as people evolved from using clubs, they began making crude bows. Archeologists have found evidence that clubs and bows were both used at the same period of time. In our country, we think of the use of the bow and arrow in connection with American Indians, but it was when people migrated from Asia that the bow came to North America.

148

{How to Tool and Lace Leather}

Materials needed: cowhide, knife or scissors, sponge, pencil or stylus, jackknife, swivel cutter.

Western leather designs are handed down from the days when the Spaniards lived in California and decorated their elaborate saddles with designs taken from the plant life around them. Beautiful as those designs are, there is no reason to feel that they are any better than those you might make using your own ideas. That's what the Spaniards did when they came to this country. Before that, leather designs had been mostly geometric designs. This was because people thought that if you made a picture of the exact plant, you would bring evil days to the plant!

After making a plan for a project, select your leather, usually cowhide, and carefully arrange the pattern pieces for the best use of the size and shape leather you have. A simple rectangle cut to use as a bookmark makes an ideal beginning project, but you may want to go beyond that.

① DRAW A DESIGN AND SHAPE ON PAPER. CUT OUT SHAPE.

At any rate, make a design for tooling and for your pattern pieces on paper. You may cut your leather pieces either with a knife or scissors depending on the thickness. Trace around the edges of the pattern pieces laid out on the flesh side. Make sure

that when you turn them over to use with the grain, they will not be backwards. Cut the piece out.

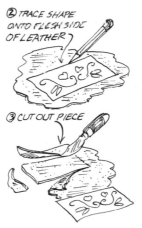

② TRACE SHAPE ONTO FLESH SIDE OF LEATHER

③ CUT OUT PIECE

Now sponge from the flesh side of the first piece you wish to tool. Make sure not to wet the leather too much, making damp spots show through to the other side, but make it wet enough to thoroughly soften the piece. You should not be able to squeeze any water out of it. If you do get it too wet, let it dry completely before working again.

④ DAMPEN LEATHER WITH WET SPONGE

FLESH SIDE

After dampening the leather, place the matching design piece of paper onto the grain side and draw firmly over the design lines, not the texture part, if

any. You can use a pencil, or a tool available for that purpose (a stylus), or a sturdy knitting needle. If you use a pencil, hold it at an angle and be careful not to mark the leather with the lead. A line will appear in the softened leather that is actually a dent in the surface.

PAPER PATTERN

LEATHER — GRAIN SIDE UP.

⑤ PRESS IN DESIGN WITH PENCIL OR STYLUS.

(DESIGN IS DENTED INTO SURFACE)

Never go back over your tracing. Leave your lines clear. Now you are ready to carve, if your design calls for it. You will need a special tool for this called a swivel cutter. I suppose your jackknife could be used but, if possible, learn to use the swivel cutter. This is used to follow the design you have traced in your leather and carve it out. It cuts a fine line into the leather. Cut with strokes moving toward you! With the flat edge of a jackknife or a spoon handle, press the leather along one side of this cut line to make a beveled look. It's a good idea to practice all three of these things — wetting, tracing, cutting — before working on your project, if you have an extra scrap of leather.

149

SWIVEL CUTTER

BLADE   FINGER POSITIONER

② CUT TOWARD YOURSELF

① PRESS ALONG CUT LINE WITH A DULL EDGE.

The design work you have seen on pretty leather products is done with special leather tools for special effects known as seeding, veining, beveling, shading, and so on. With a little imagination and practice and dampening your leather, you can use home tools for your own effects. The edge of a tack hammer, nails, and screw heads for repeat areas are all possible choices.

(DAMP LEATHER)

One more thing you might want to know how to do is *lacing*. It's a good finish when putting two edges together, even if you have used glue, too, for strength. Lacing is done with fine strips of leather shaved thin and made round or flat. If you use round lacing, be careful as you work that you aren't twisting it as the work will never lie right. If using flat lacing, one side will be shiny, so manipulate it carefully to keep the same surface showing throughout.

There are many styles and stitches used for lacing. Some designs are more important to the finished work than the carving. All of them are worked through evenly spaced holes punched or cut in the leather, and the best work is done with a needle because the raw edges of the leather bend and fray. Waxing lace with beeswax makes it work better.

A simple running stitch is actually lacing, as is whipping, but the one usually thought of in using the term *lacing* is named the *single cordovan*. This is named after the Spanish town, Cordova, where much fine leather has always been made and worked.

LEATHER LACING

① BEESWAX

LARGE NEEDLE HELPS

OR TAPERED END

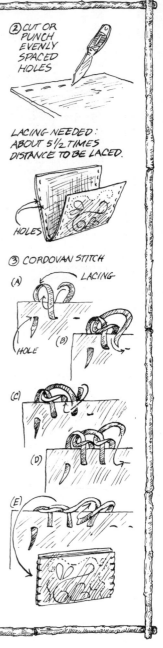

② CUT OR PUNCH EVENLY SPACED HOLES

LACING NEEDED: ABOUT 5½ TIMES DISTANCE TO BE LACED.

HOLES

③ CORDOVAN STITCH

(A)   LACING

HOLE   (B)

(C)

(D)

(E)

The account of Ishi, a Yahi Indian, provides a clue to that migration — a clue that was living up until his death in 1916. There are three different traditional positions for firing a bow. One of these is the Mongolian, and when the lone Indian, Ishi, was found, it was discovered that the position he used for firing his bow was almost exactly that used by the ancient Mongolian people. All other tribes had long since modified and adapted to the requirements necessary for firing from horseback or canoes.

In Europe, archery was refined and even became the sport of kings, but gradually people here chose not to use the long bow of England and Europe, and the one known now as the flat bow became the choice. Indians and Eskimos didn't always have perfect wood to use, and so ingenious bows were made out of the materials at hand. Bows have been found made out of pieces of whalebone, horn, and driftwood. One of the most famous was made by the Plains Indians out of strips of mountain-sheep horn glued together and bound with sinew. Glue for bow making was made from various things, even boiled salmon skins! Early North American bows were so valued for their strength that an Indian would trade as many as two good horses for one bow.

Arrows and arrowheads are just as interesting as bows because the best wood and rock were often hard to find and were treasured and traded. One of the best rocks for making arrowheads is obsidian, and all through history we can find old trade routes where obsidian was one of the sought-after materials. It looks like black glass and is extremely hard. The art of making arrows and arrowheads become so developed that individual men could be identified from the arrowheads alone, by the way the materials were handles and the individual techniques used.

Another of the very old crafts which was developed first for protection and shelter and then for pleasure and making useful articles is leathercraft. Remains of old civilizations all over the world show that as people evolved, they gradually learned how to use hides and to preserve them. American Indians had their own ideas about leather; people in the Middle Ages had theirs; Egyptians, too, had a method for leather preservation. If a hide is not tanned, it will rot. This is because it is organic. The nitrogen content in the animal cells will cause a hide to decompose. Gradually all different people and tribes figured out how to stop that. And one of the common old ingredients used again and again all over is the animal itself; that is, the brains and liver. These were made into a paste or solution. Even today they are used in some of our big commercial tanneries instead of chemicals.

In the recipe for tanning a hide at home, the fur is left on. In leathermaking the hair side is usually removed. For tooling and making articles of leather, that is the kind of leather you choose. The Indians where I live remove that hair by a long soak in saltwater or sometimes by rolling up the hide with the hair covered in wood ashes and a little water. This, I suppose, is like what is done commercially in the lime vats. After a couple of days, the hide is unrolled and the hair is scraped off.

Hide for leather tooling and making belts, purses, and saddles, has two layers. The side which the hair was scraped from is called the *grain* side. This also holds the glue material you try to remove when you tan the skin. The underskin, or *flesh* side, is the tough, rough side. Tooling and finishing is done on the *grain* side.

Better Than We Found It

All of these basic crafts are close to nature and the out-of-doors. Seeing and being ready to use and appreciate all the abundance provided by gardens and yards and woods and fields and animal friends can occupy an entire lifetime. Then

{How to Tan a Prime Hide}

Materials needed: animal hide (rabbit, squirrel, goat, sheep, deer), alum, saltpeter, salt, newspapers, scraper or dull knife, detergent, borax, neat's-foot oil, sandpaper.

A prime hide is in top condition with no blemishes and full maturity of coat and skin. Perhaps you would like to know just a little about what happens to a skin that changes it from a stiff, hard piece to a nice, soft and usable leather. It is really called *tawing,* but most people use the words *taw* and *tan* to mean the same thing now. The word *tan* comes from the tannic acid which is found in lots of plants in nature, but especially in live oak trees. Tannic acid is important in tanning and tawing.

The important thing is to replace the matter that is in the skin cells. This matter is almost a glue — very stiff, and it must be removed before the skin can become soft. In this recipe, the borax and detergent make this glue into a kind of gelatin so that the underskin can be peeled, and the cells can be broken down and softened by the rubbing. The more rubbing, the softer your finished skin! The alum and salt mixture pulls the liquid out of the skin so that the cells don't hold any more glue or gelatin. Then more rubbing and scraping makes it even softer than before.

A hide can be either fresh or frozen. If frozen, thaw in lukewarm water.

Step 1: Wash: this can be done in a washing machine. Use 1 cup borax, 1 cup detergent, and cold water. Agitate for 15 minutes for small skins, 30 minutes for goats and larger. Rinse twice in cold water.

① WASH HIDE.

COLD WASH → 15–30 MIN.
COLD RINSE → TWICE

Step 2: Towel dry the skin and lay it hair side down, on an old rug or towel. Rub hard, especially at the edges, to loosen underskin and fat. Now try to peel the loose underskin and scrape off any excess fat with a blunt knife. The skin *must* be free of *any* fat and meat.

TOWEL DRY HIDE
②

← HAIR SIDE DOWN

OLD RUG OR TOWEL ↗

③ RUB HARD TO LOOSEN FAT.

④ USE BLUNT KNIFE TO PEEL AND SCRAPE OFF LOOSE SKIN AND FAT.

Step 3: Hang the skin up with skin sides together to dry the hair. Don't leave it up more than a few hours because odor develops.

⑤

← HIDE, HANGING WITH SKIN SIDES TOGETHER

Step 4: Place the hide, hair side down, on a layer of six to eight newspapers. Cover the skin side with a mixture made up of 1 cup powdered alum, 1 cup saltpeter, and 1 cup plain table salt. You can get the alum and saltpeter at a drugstore. Rub the mixture in. Cover the skin with more layers of newspaper and roll it up tightly. Don't allow the salt mixture to get on the hair. Store the hide in a cool place.

153

OPEN. RUB MIXTURE INTO
ANY SHINY PLACES.
ROLL UP AGAIN.

⑥

ALUM
1 CUP

SALT PETER
1 CUP

TABLE SALT
1 CUP

NEWSPAPER

HIDE, HAIR SIDE DOWN.
MIXTURE MUST NOT TOUCH
HAIR.
RUB MIXTURE
INTO
SKIN ⑦

COVER WITH MORE
NEWSPAPERS

ROLL UP ⑧

STORE IN A COOL PLACE.

Step 5: Two days later check the mixture on the hide. Shiny spots must be covered with more mixture. Roll up and store again. Goat skins take about ten days to cure, rabbits less.

Step 6: Curing is finished when the skin is *white* when scraped with a blunt knife. Unroll the skin and place it on a rounded surface, if possible; then start scraping with a blunt knife. Finish the whole surface this way. It will be snowy white and not very stiff. A final finish can be done with an electric sander or by rubbing with sandpaper. Doing the sanding gives a suede finish. Oil, such as neat's-foot oil, is sometimes rubbed in too.

No tanning is easy, but the results of a lot of rubbing and scraping are worth it and give you something that nobody else

⑩ SCRAPE WITH
DULL KNIFE.

RUB WITH SANDPAPER
(ON BLOCK)
OR USE
ELECTRIC
SANDER

can imitate. Each hide is different, and they are all useful. If you goof on your first efforts to tan, cut the skin into strips and use it for rawhide. Rawhide is useful for many, many projects.

In the early years of our country the fur trading industry was one of the things that lured men to the western territories. They trapped and skinned their catches and canoed the waterways back to towns where bundles of furs were traded for huge amounts of money. It was a dangerous business, and the men who lived that way had to be tough and clever. They learned a great deal from the Indians who had used hides for everything from houses to babies' blankets.

When we cousins camped *up north* each summer, we were always presented with a gift to take home. Each one was made of buckskin and usually was decorated with beads. Gloves, moccasins, and vests were some of these treasures.

The buckskin was the softest thing imaginable. I wish I knew how it was made, though of course I never will! When I asked, my friend just smiled! Buckskin is made from deerhide and has no hair on it. It is lovely, soft, and either white or tan, depending on what it is used for.

Some recipes are known and can be found in books written especially about tanning or Indian crafts. Just the same, I am sure each tribe had its own special secret, because buckskin is not the same everywhere. Also, the more people I have met who tan, the more different ways to tan I have found. The one I have written here doesn't use dangerous or hard-to-find chemicals so I, personally, have found it a good old favorite to use at home.

instead of wasting, we learn to treasure, nurture, and to cherish. People of other times come to life in our minds and become sources of wonder.

One of the most surprising and interesting classes I ever took was at the University of Wisconsin and taught by a wonderful lady named Helen Allen. It was, of all things, the history of embroidery. Imagine! But think! Where did the color and thread come from? Why did people do it? How did they first learn?

In my imagination I found myself slogging across the world with Marco Polo and reporting to the king's court about those delicate Oriental decorations. Wars were fought and civilizations flourished because of their command of color! *Color!* How could people have cared that much! I think part of it was that they could see and were aware of what nature gave in treasured portions to those who knew her secrets. Like people of old, we learn to know how the world can help us to live and enjoy ourselves, and like people of old we have the choice, still, to use it all up or to leave the world better than we found it because we were here. That's hard. Can you do it?

❧ More Books to Read ❧

Amsden, Charles. *Navaho Weaving: Its Technique and Its History.* Fine Arts Press, Santa Ana, Ca., 1969. The standard work on this subject.

Birrell, Verla. *Textile Arts.* Shocken Books, New York, 1973. A big section on all kinds of weaving techniques; a great resource.

Boy Scouts of America. *Revised Handbook for Boys.* New Brunswick, N. J., 1940. Still a great all-around handbook.

Brooklyn Botanical Garden Record. *Plants and Gardens, Vol. 20, No. 3: A Handbook.* 1968. This has standard dye references; for ages eight and up. Botanical Gardens address: 1000 Washington Ave., Brooklyn, N. Y. 11225.

Burgess, Thornton W. *Burgess Book of Nature Lore.* Bonanza Books, New York, 1975. Burgess will always be interesting and beautiful for all ages.

Candy, Robert. *Nature Notebook.* Riverside Press, Houghton Mifflin Co., Cambridge, Mass., 1953. An actual notebook by Robert Candy and his boy.

Condon, Geneal. *The Art of Flower Preservation.* Sunset Books, Lane Book Co., Menlo Park, Ca., 1962. Thorough and inexpensive.

Davenport, Elsie. *Your Handspinning.* Craft and Hobby Book Service, Pacific Grove, Ca., 1964. Pictures and good information. Address: P. O. Box 626, Pacific Grove, Ca. 95950.

Fat Cabin Press. *Tanning.* Fat Cabin Press, Arcata, Ca. A short easy pamphlet — good.

Garriott, Edward. *Weather Folklore.* U. S. Govt. Printing Office Report, Grand Rivers Books, Detroit, Mich. Interesting and fun.

Hammett, Catherine. *Your Own Book of Campcraft.* Pocket Books, Inc., New York, 1960. Easy to use and helpful.

Hart, Carol and Dan. *Natural Basketry.* Watson Guptil Publications, New York, 1976. Complete, easy to use, good pictures.

Hunt, Ben. *Ben Hunt's Big Indiancraft Book.* Bruce Publishing Co., Milwaukee, Wisc., 1942. Ben Hunt's books are all a treat to use and read — a creative resource.

Leach, Bernard. *A Potter's Book.* Trans-Atlantic Arts, Inc., Hollywood, Fla., 1962. Every serious potter owns this book.

157

Lesch, Alma. *Vegetable Dyeing.* Watson Guptil Publications, New York, 1970. Excellent and easy.

Nauman, Rose and Hull, Raymond. *Off-Loom Weaving Book.* Charles Scribner's Sons, New York, 1973. Easy to use and inspiring, good pictures.

Phillips, Mary Walker. *Macrame: Step-by-Step.* Golden Press, Western Publishing Co., Inc., Racine, Wisconsin, 1970. Pictures and easy projects.

Pringle, L., ed. *Discovering the Outdoors.* Natural History Press, Garden City, N. Y., 1969.

Ress, Etta Schneider. *Community of Living Things in Field and Meadow, Vol. 1.* Nat'l Audubon Society Creative Educational Society, Inc., Mankato, Minn., 1956. Pictures and identifications.

Seton, Julia. *American Indian Arts.* Ronald Press, 1962. Julia and Ernest Thompson Seton books are all fun and interesting — outdoor and Indian works.

Tod, Osma Gallinger. *Earth Basketry.* Bonanza Books, New York, 1972. One of the best basket books, out of print, but easy to find in libraries.

Tod, Osma Gallinger and Benson, Oscar H. *Weaving with Reeds and Fibers.* Dover Publications, Inc., New York, 1975.

Wigginton, Eliot, ed. *Foxfire Books.* Anchor Books, Doubleday and Co., Inc., Garden City, New York, 1972.

Znamierowski, Nell. *Weaving: Step-by-Step.* Golden Press, Western Publishing Co., Inc., Racine, Wisc., 1967. Easy with simple projects.

⟩[Index of Crafts]⟨

159